Where Bones Dance

Terrace Books, a division of the University of Wisconsin Press,
takes its name from the Memorial Union Terrace, located at
the University of Wisconsin–Madison. Since its inception in 1907,
the Wisconsin Union has provided a venue for students, faculty, staff,
and alumni to debate art, music, politics, and the issues of the day.
It is a place where theater, music, drama, dance, outdoor activities,
and major speakers are made available to the campus and the community.
To learn more about the Union, visit www.union.wisc.edu.

Where Bones Dance

An English Girlhood, An African War

Nina Newington

Terrace Books
A trade imprint of the University of Wisconsin Press

Terrace Books
An imprint of the University of Wisconsin Press
1930 Monroe Street
Madison, Wisconsin 53711

www.wisc.edu/wisconsinpress/

3 Henrietta Street
London WC2E 8LU, England

1 3 5 4 2

Printed in the United States of America

Library of Congress Cataloging-in-Publication Data
Newington, Nina, 1958–
Where bones dance : an English girlhood,
an African war / Nina Newington.
p. cm.
ISBN 0-299-22260-8 (alk. paper)
1. Children—Fiction. 2. British—Nigeria—Fiction.
3. Nigeria—History—1960—Fiction.
4. Nigeria—History—Civil War, 1967–1970—Fiction. I. Title.
PR6114.E946W47 2007
823′.92—dc22 2006031769

For all the anonymous saviors,
and in particular
Christine,
whose last name I do not know

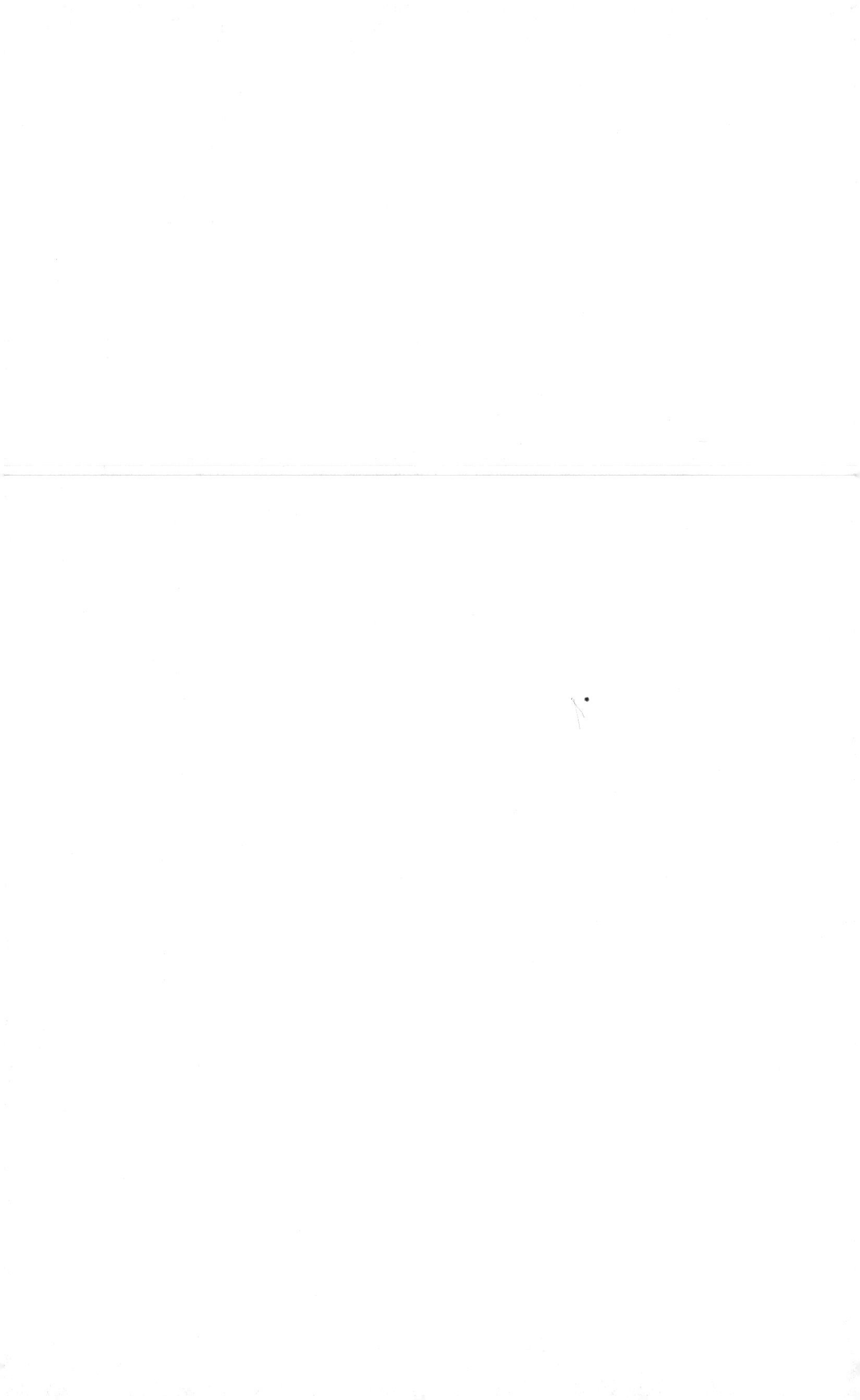

Any sorrow can be borne if a story can be told about it.

Isak Dinesen

Some events do take place but are not true; others are—although they never occurred.

Elie Wiesel

Contents

Cycle II: The English Ibeji

Cycle III: The Mosquito King

Cycle IV: Harvest of Ghosts

Preface

I lived in Nigeria from when I was seven until I was ten but, before writing this book, I had almost no conscious memory of that time, or indeed of the first twelve years of my life. There were things I knew had happened because they were a part of the family stories my mother told, but these were far from being direct recollections of my own experiences.

The first time I wrote about Nigeria the story startled me with its immediacy. It came from an unknown place inside myself. It was the first short story I ever got published and it contained the germ of this book. I made a list then of incidents, things, and people I associated with my time in Nigeria. Several years later, during a residency at an artists' colony, I started writing from the list, choosing whatever item drew me that day.

The stories came as if they had been gathering inside for years. Beyond the small effort each morning of launching myself from whichever point on the list had drawn me, I did not try to make anything happen. My only work was the moment to moment work of being true to the words and images as they came.

As I wrote I was startled again by the vividness with which Nigeria became present to me. The sensory perceptions were so acute I doubted I could be inventing them. Nigerian artifacts such as the wooden figures of twins came into my mind with names—Ibejis—I would later check and find accurate.

In this way writing returned memory to me, and yet it was vital to me that I did not have to make what I was writing objectively true. In writing I was discovering truth. I could only do that by refusing to fret about whether what I wrote was actually true or not, so I gave myself, in the writing of this book, complete permission to lie.

As I wrote I found I was writing the story of a child to whom truth, fact, sense were desperately important but who nonetheless told stories she knew weren't true. She told so many stories she lost track of what was true and what wasn't. The particular panic that gripped her then was one of the few feelings I'd always remembered. I knew that girl was me.

Some of the lies I told as a child were of the ordinary, boastful sort, but some were an attempt to tell truths that were at the time (and for many years afterwards) unspeakable. I have come to believe that in each of us the truth wants to tell itself. Often it can only do so through fiction.

Acknowledgments

Quotations from:

"Brown Skin Girl," traditional Calypso
Journal of an expedition to explore the course and termination of the Niger, with a narrative of a voyage down the river to its termination, by Richard and John Lander (London and New York, 1832)
"Daffodils," by William Wordsworth

Sections of this book have appeared in the following journals and anthologies: *The American Voice, Sinister Wisdom, Common Lives/Lesbian Lives, Ikon, Jo's Girls,* ed. Christian McEwen (Beacon Press, 1997); and *Resurgent: New Writings by Women,* ed. Camille Norton and Lou Robinson (Urbana: University of Illinois Press, 1992).

Thanks to Gloria Anzaldúa, who opened the doors of writing for me; to the now defunct Cummington Community of the Arts, which gave me first a residency and then a job; to Joan Larkin for years of fabulous conversation and a vital lead; to Diane Cleaver, my agent, sadly dead now, who believed in this book and represented it even though it was unlikely ever to make her any money. Thanks to the Reverend Rich Fournier for walking by my side through the valley of the shadow. And thanks to all the friends who have read and commented on this manuscript: Carol Potter, Dee Dee Niswonger, Dvora Cohen, Emerald O'Leary, Moira Gentry, to name only a few. For scanning the old, typed manuscript, everlasting gratitude to Maureen "Mickie" Conroy and, for lying on it whenever possible, exasperated love to Sido, Trouble, Ben, Sylvie, and Stevie. Finally, special thanks to Alexa Jaffurs, who read the manuscript between lambing and haying, researched the chronology of the Biafran war, and is my companion and my delight.

Cycle I

*

Good Snake

1965–1968

Lagos

Lagos. Lagos. The door swings open. The breath of the jungle scorches my skin. Sweat and shit and tar and green, metallic as blood, the smell floods the plane, drowning the staleness of chicken and gin. The jungle pours into my lungs. I am breathing heat. The runway is far below, shimmering like it's underwater. There are silver steps, long drop one to one to one. Lagos, Lagos, Lagos, I say. I slip. The metal burns my calf.

Lines

My hands circle Christine's arm, thumbs touching where the skin is soft. My fingers won't reach around her biceps. I trace the ridges on her forearms, too straight for accident, too regular. They are like mountain ranges seen from the air. I want to touch the lines on her face, her Ibo lines. She tells how the women cut the child's skin with a knife. They mix mud with the blood. There's earth in her arms, in her face. It is for beauty and strength. It must hurt. "Where do you come from?" I ask.

"Omomwe," she says, "a village three hundred miles east of here, past Enugu. My husband and my children live there, as well as my aunts and sisters."

"Why did you come to Lagos? Don't you like them?"

She looks at me and shakes her head.

"Well then why can't you go back there?"

"If I go there we will all be hungry."

I look at her face. I want to ask more questions. I saw her laugh one time, her breasts shook and her hands spread wide. She stamped her foot. I never saw anyone laugh like that before. Mostly she looks like she is guarding a secret place in her mind and she only lets herself visit it sometimes but she always knows it's there. I want to know what it is.

Beach

My father pulls the engine cord. He is six foot four. He bends his knees and pulls. The whole boat rocks and the brown water goes out in ripples. Everything smells of petrol. There is a skin on the water, shining blue and pink like the bubbles he taught us to blow in the bath. He squatted down by the side, rubbed soap in my hand, made me clench it in a fist and then slowly, slowly open my forefinger and thumb in an O. "Blow now, gently," he said. The film of soap went out like a long tongue and then it became a perfect little circle with rainbows and floated away. He blew huge ones which stayed long and wobbly and quivered in the air before they popped. We go through the harbor past the tall grey ships and wood bobbing in the water and a pink doll without any arms, covered in tar. We go up Badgieri creek. It is a green-brown tunnel. The trees are reflected in the water. There's no sky.

"Look," says Bill, "there's a crocodile."

"Another one," I say. "You're always seeing crocodiles."

His mouth moves like a cow chewing cud, but fast now. He is so excited he stands up and blows a big pink bubble like a cartoon character about to say something, and the wind blows it in his hair.

I say, "See, it's not, it's just an old tree."

My mother is fussing at him now, she'll have to cut the gum out of his hair but soon we eat ginger biscuits and the creek is wide grey green and the jungle on the right side is thick and purple and black. Faces look out at me. I see their eyes. But when I look back, they're gone. We go on and then we reach the place where there's a little wooden jetty. There are people there already. My father cuts the engine, swinging the boat to the left. They wade in the water and take the rope and tie it up on the jetty.

We get out and my father passes things and the people take the things on their heads, the red and white ice bucket and the food chest and the towels and the water and then we walk down the path. I take my flip-flops off because they give me blisters and the sand is cool enough under the palm trees and the creeping plants don't prickle much. The sand slides through between my toes. Off to the right a man is sewing a fishing net, and a boy up a tree with a rope around his waist cuts a coconut. He throws it down onto the sand. He cuts four, then he comes down. He cuts the tops off with his machete and my father gives him money. The coconut is big and green. It is smooth between my hands. I tip it up. I tip my whole head back and drink from it. The milk is clean and woody, sweet a little. Mine has lots of jelly in it. I ask the boy will he cut it in half? and he does. There is white then brown then a hairy reddish layer like a nest and then the hard green skin.

My mother says, "We've never found coconuts like the ones we had in the Philippines when you were a baby."

I eat the jelly, making my fingers into a spoon. The boy's stomach is round like a coconut, like he ate a whole one, but his arms are skinny and his eyes are red. There's a fly on his nose but he doesn't make it go away. Bill wants to climb a palm tree too.

My mother says, "Little monkey."

My father says, "Later."

Now the sand is hot and there aren't any more roots and prickly leaves and the ocean makes all the noise. I can see forever. "See that canoe, it's full of fish, let me see, there's a hammerhead shark and two barracuda and—"

"You can't see that far."

"Want to bet?"

"We'll see when he comes in."

My father pays the people. I want to run into the sea but we have to wait until he talks to the fishermen to see if it is safe today. I am standing on the sand, all I can hear is the ocean. Every month somebody drowns. My father is smiling so I take off my shirt and I run down to the water and a wave comes up to my knees. It sucks at my feet and all the sand goes out from under my heels. I wait. I look down at my chest, the bony line down the middle, one nipple on either side, small like seeds. Right after a wave comes in I run into the water and I dive through the one that's curling up and I swim hard before it pulls me back to the beach. I swim, then I'm floating on the big waves like Popeye on the back of the whale. Sharks swim under my toes. I am riding the waves like sea horses cantering and now I want to catch one when it breaks and fly on it like a fish, a flying fish, there's one, no, there's one, I can see a big one coming. When it's right behind me I swim and swim till I feel it pick me up. I hold my arms straight out in front of me and I open my eyes. I see black and white and green and blue all jumbled up and I am flying into them, into the middle of colors, and then the sand is scratching at my belly. I run out of the water before the next wave comes. I wipe the salt from my eyes. I pull up my bikini bottoms. They're full of pebbles. I feel them there, hard and little.

My eyes are stinging. Up the beach I see my mother lying by the blue and white umbrella. It's like I'm looking through a telescope. I can see the pores in her skin like the holes termites make in wood, tunnels I could crawl into. The tunnels are slimy, they smell of mushrooms and fish. When she moves the walls quiver like in an earthquake. My belly heaves. I can't move. I'm going to be sick. Stop looking. I make my eyes go up. There's a kite turning figures of eight over and over. Look at the sea. It's like skin moving over bones. It's not. It's the sea. I'll dive back in. I wait for the moment between waves. The waves are taller than me. They're taller than my father. When they curl up at the top I see fish swimming in them.

School

I'm sitting at one end of the bench. The slats are cutting into my thighs. The Nigerian children are on the next bench which is a long way away. They are eating out of Disney lunchboxes too but I know what they are eating is funny. They eat their food with their hands and it smells of pepper but then I see they're eating sandwiches. Matthew who is sitting next to me is eating a peanut butter and jelly sandwich. I can smell the thick peanut smell. I'm eating ham and tomato.

"Tomahto," says Matthew and the two girls on my bench say it too. They will say it over and over. "Tomahto. Doo yew have a butler." I don't know the girls' names, only Matthew's. We're in the clever half of third grade. He's top of the class but I'm going to be top. Suddenly he is gone and I see teams are forming to play Red Rover. I want to play. The Nigerian children are playing hopscotch by their bench and not even looking where all the noise is. I get up and walk toward the teams but a little off course so if no one speaks to me I can just keep walking like I'm going somewhere. To the bathroom. But instead I hold my breath and walk into them and somebody says, "Who's left? You're on our team," and so I am and I hold the hands of people on either side, their hand around my wrist and mine around theirs. A big boy runs at us and I feel my arms pulling and then going loose and all our team looks at the boy and girl who let him through. When it's their turn the leader says, "Red Rover, Red Rover, Let the Limey fly over" and I step out. Facing me is a girl wearing glasses. Her twin sister, Caroline, is in my class. She is Oriental. I run into her arm. She doesn't let go. It's like her arm stretches and stretches and then it just snaps back in place and I fall over and all her team laughs at me. When it is her turn she runs at me and I don't let go either. She looks at me and squares her shoulders. She says, "Hey, you think you're tough." I grin and say, "Yeah, reckon I am," like the man in 'The Virginian.' That's how come I'm here with her now, holding her hand, our elbows on the table.

"Ready?"

"Mmhmm."

Neither of us is moving. I can feel the sweat on the side of my nose. I feel my hand begin to go but I breathe and push her back.

"One. Two. Three." At ten it will be a draw. "Eight." Her hand goes. "I won," I say. She is turned around. She is looking at a woman who is so small she is like a bird that hops from foot to foot.

"This is my mother," says Helen, "Mrs. Lee."

"Oh," I say, "Hello. My name is Anna Stevenson," and I duck my head.

"You're Jack Stevenson's daughter."

"Yes."

"You're welcome to come over after school one afternoon. Ask your mother if you may."

"Oh yes, thank you," I say, trying to see Helen's face. Maybe she doesn't want me to. She's kicking the dirt with her sneakers.

"Yeah," she says, "and we'll wrestle again. Best of three." She goes to their car. Caroline is there. Caroline is a girl girl. There is a little boy with a crew cut too. I look around for Bill. He's sitting under the table with his hands down his shorts. I wonder if he was sitting there all the time we were wrestling.

"Where's Mum?" he says.

"She'll be here in a minute."

Christine

The thorns tear my legs. I crawl under the bougainvillea whose flowers are a flight of crimson butterflies. I crawl into the shade. My eyes pick out brown, yellow, khaki, pools of color running into each other, a coil thickening, thicker than my arm, coils inward: snake.

"Christine. Christine. Christine." With the machete she comes running. "Snake. There's a snake."

"It is a good snake. It has eaten a rat so it sleeps. We don't kill this snake," she says.

Dave

Up in Helen's room I walk around. There isn't anything to look at. Everything is square and white and clean.

She says, "Do you know Judo?"

"No," I say. I will never catch up.

Out of her closet Helen takes baggy white trousers and a jacket. I feel them and they are thick and soft.

"This is a ghi," she says. "Dad says it's part of our heritage. Well, Tae Kwon Do is, but Judo is what they teach here."

I feel my face get red and shiny and like it is bigger than me. I can't make the picture go away: the shiny pink sash and the white dress sticking out around my knees, Mrs. Hawkins's voice going "gracefully, gracefully, girls" and then I am high in the casuarina tree in my jeans and then I am the tree, my skin all scaly and brown. Afterwards my mother was late and I had to stand in the courtyard under the flame tree which had pink fluffy flowers and I wanted to kick it and kick it.

"My name is Jake," I say. "I am a marine."

Helen says, "My name is Dave. It's a code name. I am a spy."

She sticks out her hand and I shake it hard.

"Will you teach me Judo?"

"Stand over here."

I go to the foot of the bed. She does something with her hands and feet, slides one arm under my elbows and then I'm falling over on the bed but I hold onto her and pull her down too and then we are twisting and pushing and she gets her knee between my legs but I am on top. I hold her leg tight with my knees. I hold her arms down with my hands. I push down. I want to keep pushing. She is pushing up. My heart is beating very slowly in my belly. Dave pulls her arms loose. She is pushing my shoulders away. Her other leg comes around on the side of my leg and then she is sitting on top of me, my leg between her legs and her hands on my shoulders and I can see the wind in her face like she is riding a horse in the desert. She is moving up and down only it feels like water hitting the side of a boat and she is a sailor looking far away at the sky. I get slower and slower like a long wave pulling up and up and then it is the wind tangling in my chest and a scream starting in my belly and like a hand inside my body as big as my body clenching in a fist and I push her off of me. I have to lie there very still until I get back inside me.

Dave says, "That wasn't Judo, that was wrestling. In Judo you know what you are going to do. You learn different moves."

I think I'm going to cry. I look at her very seriously. I say, "What happened to you when you were born?" She looks in my eyes. "Who sat on your face?" I say. "Who made it flat?"

She is still looking at me. She doesn't smile.

"Say that again," she says, "I'll sit on your face and I'll squash it good."

I look down. "Yeah," I say, "Yeah, Dave."

"Jake," she says.

"Let's go outside. Let's get Jerry and Bill."

Red

"You only like your family, don't you? Just like your old Mum. All the rest are mean and nasty, aren't they?" Red wags his tail. "Bite 'em?"

Red wags his tail some more. At the same time he sits down. It looks like he will fall over. Instead he puts his left paw on my mother's knee.

She takes it and kisses it. "What a rake you are. What a handsome dog."

He looks up at her. He is panting. His tail swishes across the floor. It sweeps an ant clear across two tiles but the ant doesn't let go of its crumb. Red keeps lifting his paw and putting it down on my mother's knee. His thing is sticking out. It is bright pink and glistening. At the end there is a little blob of yellow stuff.

My mother is rubbing him in between his ears. "You devil of a dog," she says, "you know why I picked you? Because you bit my hand. If it wasn't for me they'd have put you to sleep. Do you know that?"

There is a red mark on her knee from his paw.

My father puts down his paper. "You'd better be getting dressed, darling, or we'll be late."

"Another cocktail party," she says to Red.

"We have to put in an appearance," says my father. "We won't stay long."

My mother bends over Red and whispers in his ear.

"Come on, Anna love."

She gets up. Red rolls over on his back, his tail still wagging so the back half of his body twists from side to side. He looks at my mother. She rubs her foot on his belly.

"You dirty dog," she says, "look at your tassel hanging out."

My father picks up the newspaper again.

She goes inside, closing the screen door behind her.

Red carries on lying there. I go and rub his chest. My father puts the newspaper down again. He looks at his watch and stands up. The suit he is wearing is creamy grey linen. It was made by a tailor in Hong Kong before I was born. He wears a brown belt and his brown shoes shine. The jacket is hanging over the back of his chair. He looks down. His shoes look very long and pointy next to Red who is still lying there with his paws in the air.

"Come on," says my father, "come on, Red." He goes to the corner by the house and picks up a ball. The ball is orange and blue plastic with holes in it. He goes to the edge of the veranda. "Red," he says, waving the ball at him. Red gets up. My father pauses, holding the ball high in the air, then he throws it. "Fetch," he says.

Red stands there wagging his tail. The ball rolls into the bougainvillea. I crawl under the thorns and get it. I throw it to my father. I don't throw it far enough but he runs and catches it. He goes right up to Red and holds the ball under his nose. "Fetch," he says. He pretends to throw it. Red wags his tail. He watches the ball in my father's hand. He prances a little. "Fetch," says my father and he throws the ball. Red sits down.

I run and stop it before it rolls into the lagoon. When I turn to throw it my mother is on the veranda. Here it smells of swamp. The veranda is far away. My father is looking down at her. She is wearing a dark green dress. It floats around her. Her hair looks very black and shiny against my father's creamy grey jacket. He puts his arm around her and they walk into the house. He closes the screen door again.

Red gets up and walks slowly around the side of the house. He pisses on the washing pole. I put the ball down in the corner. My mother's perfume hangs in the air, lilies and gin. I sit down in the big rattan chair and read the newspaper.

Daniel

"Daniel has a photographic memory," says my mother. "I can show him a recipe once and he can repeat it to me word for word. He reads French too."

"What a find."

"You should taste his meringues. He was trained by the French ambassador's wife."

"You lucky dog," says Peg, giggling, "I bet the Frogs are fuming." The way her cheeks are blotched makes her look like a toad. "But isn't he a Hausa? What do you do on Fridays?"

"He's a Christian Hausa."

Daniel is tall and thin and dark dark brown. He looks like he grew up in a dry country. I can see him walking in white with a long staff like Joseph leading the donkey. He clicks his tongue like a camera when he looks at a book. He's taking pictures of everything he sees. His mind must be full of them. Was he always like that? Does he have pictures of the desert he looks at at night? How does he find the picture he wants?

"He has seven sons and they're all either doctors or lawyers. He put each of them through university on a cook's wages. Can you imagine?" says my mother.

I don't go in the kitchen when he's there. Once he chased me out of the kitchen with a carving knife. I climbed the washing pole and he pretended he couldn't reach me.

Relations

They are pink and wrinkly and something smells too sweet. He is moving his head back and forth and around without the rest of his body and he keeps laughing. She is bending down toward me with her arms stretched out. Her arms are loose and white. I am walking towards her. I don't want to kiss her cheek, it will come off on my lips. I walk past her into the garden. Grandpop already has Bill. He is moving the flat of his hand back and forth across his hair. Mum and Dad are standing facing Ma and Grandpop, and Bill is in between. Nobody moves. My mother is smiling. Gabriel comes in carrying a tray with glasses of Pimms and lemonade and my grandfather has a Heineken.

"I beg your pardon," says my grandmother.

"Would you like to look at the garden?" says my mother.

She said they would bring us presents. Ma and Grandpop are rich but they didn't used to be. We mustn't talk like them but if we are careful they will give us money.

"It was a jungle," says my mother, walking out onto the veranda, "one dingy rose bed, the rest a jungle."

"Oh I love roses," says my grandmother. "Nothing like an English rose, though of course ours will be almost over by the time we get back."

"It's such fun gardening here," says my mother. "You stick a twig in the ground and six months later it is a giant bush. All the oleander I planted myself, and most of the bougainvillea. Beautiful, isn't it? Though of course the snakes love it too, pythons, green mambas, vipers. We have some monster, don't we darling?"

I nod and watch my mother's tongue flick the red specks of lipstick from her front teeth. "Oh yes," I say. "There's an African python that lives over there under the bougainvillea bush. I saw it yesterday. It's as tall as Dad."

"Oh really darling, don't exaggerate."

She is smiling at me.

My grandmother is holding her handbag in front of her with both hands. "Well young lady, Anna Gwyneth," she says, "will you give your grandmother a kiss now?" I look at her and then I run away to the water's edge. I can feel my mother smiling like the sun on my neck as I run and the sun is shining on the water hard and bright.

Gabriel has served the rice. He is passing the coronation chicken when my grandmother says, "Well, it certainly must be difficult, bringing up children in a primitive country. Honestly Anna, their manners are worse than the servants'."

I look at Gabriel. His face is far away and dreamy and there are two beads of sweat, one on either side of his nose.

My grandfather says too loud to my father, "Well old man, how is it here? Country's been independent what, five years? Military coups already. They're squabbling like children. How do the people feel about the Queen?"

Gabriel is walking into the kitchen. His feet make no sound on the floor. Upstairs I hear Christine making the beds in the spare room. She is plumping the pillows where my grandmother's face will lie, her face lying there alone like a mask, wrinkled and cast off like a snakeskin. A fly is dying on the Shell strip by the window. The strip is yellow and covered with bodies. Outside the pineapples are swelling on the ground and the snakes are eating rats. I heard Mum say to Dad that Gabriel smokes hemp and that is why he smiles a lot and forgets things.

"It's a good life for the children," says my mother, "plenty of fresh air and exercise. Not all that drizzle and sleet for months on end. Jack and I play golf every afternoon and now we have shares in a beach hut we go to the beach every other weekend."

"Just as well you're outdoor types," chuckles Grandpop. "I don't suppose they have any decent beer here do they, just this bottled stuff you have to freeze to get down."

"Oh yes, George couldn't live without his pub," says my grandmother. "At least you're by the sea and with lots of other English people. Poor Joan says they're out of their mind with boredom, stuck in the jungle drinking gin and playing bridge, surrounded by blacks and scared half the time for their lives."

"Oh come now," says my father, "Port Harcourt is hardly the back of beyond."

"Poor old Harold wants a bit of action too but I suppose working for B.P. was a break after Malta. I must say I think old Harold got the rough end of the deal."

Manners worse than the servants.' The bloody nerve. Honestly, darling, look at this. I'd never wear this. It's common, that's all there is to it. And I do think they might have learnt your shirt size by now. It's not as if you've shrunk in the last five years. These would fit your father. Not that you'd wear a mauve golf shirt in the first place. And ten pounds each for Bill and Anna. Do you know how much they shell out to Joan and Tom when Joan's married to that crook Harold and Juliet's rich as Croesus. Harold smarming up to your ma. Honestly. Do you know he writes to her once a week? She told me herself the moment they got here. All smiles of course. She loves it."

Dad is holding the purple shirt. His face looks like Bill's right before he cries, kind of crumpled. Ma and Grandpop are his mother and father. He looks at me and says, "I must say it was very rude of you not to kiss Ma hello. What's got into you?" I don't say anything. "Oh for God's sake, I know it's not easy seeing them again but you could try a bit harder." He's looking at me but I don't remember seeing them before.

"No," I say, "I've never seen them before." My mother is staring at him. Her eyes are wide and flat. It's like she isn't there.

"Well," he says, "it's time for you children to go to bed."

"Come on Bill," I say, and he crawls out from under the dressing table. We go out onto the landing. I shut the door. My belly is curling in a tight ball and there's a butterfly in my shoulder. I keep seeing her eyes.

"Oh darling," says her voice, "I don't know how someone as nice as you, as handsome and clever and distinguished as you, came out of that family." She giggles. I move my shoulder in a circle and I jump it up and down but the butterfly won't go away. I walk down the hallway to the spare bedroom and I say through the door, "Goodnight Ma, goodnight Grandpop," but there's no answer.

Moonflower

Tonight the moonflower will open. The power is out. I don't know what to expect, only it is something big because Bill and I are allowed to stay up late. We sit on the veranda and wait. The smell of the leopard coil and the hurricane lamp, my father's cigarette and whisky, my mother's brandy, wrap around me so tight I can hardly breathe. The breeze from the lagoon is like a wet tongue licking my face. A fly on my knee cleans its head with its arms. We've watched this bud get fatter for days and now it is happening. But everything else is the same. My father chuckles and waves his glass in a short arc away from his body, an arc traced by the cigarette he holds in that same hand, the cigarette he will soon stub out in the little silver ashtray, Kano silver. My mother bought it from the man on the bicycle who comes on Fridays and unwraps weird wooden figures with round bellies and long faces and legs like hoops, and also metal animals, a leopard my mother says, the one on the coffee table, a Benin bronze. Its eyes are wide, as if it has looked into the night for too long, and there are spots scratched on its long body. It doesn't look like a leopard except for the spots. On the sideboard in the dining room stand the wooden figures, naked, one with a long thing, a tassel, sticking up in front of it, another with breasts dyed blue. The breasts hang down to its belly. The figures look funny standing next to each other on the sideboard with its shiny brass handles, as if they don't want to be there, and once I thought if they ever hear the drums they will leave. It makes me go still inside thinking that. I can see them crossing the lagoon to the other side, moving just above the water.

My father taps his cigarette once, twice, on the cigarette case which is brown leather. He is talking about the troubles again. I think about Honnef and how when the Rhine turned to ice, children in red hats skated to school. I saw them from the bridge and I thought they were like fireflies. My mother said in Hong Kong people caught fireflies in jars and used them as lanterns and I worried that maybe they died, but on the river the red and blue and green and yellow hats were moving like ants on the march, they were all going in the same direction. It never snows in Nigeria. Red has never seen snow. I have never seen a moonflower.

"Look," says Mum, "look very carefully."

Little stripes of white are showing. When did that happen?

"It happens so slowly you can't quite see it," says my father, "but if you watch closely enough you might."

This is what I don't understand. How I'm here in the dark in this smell and it is so hot I can feel sweat running down the backs of my legs, and before I was in Germany and before that in England and before that in Hong Kong and before that I was nowhere. I am watching the bud very carefully. I want to see it happen. It isn't enough when I forget to look and then when I remember it has moved. It's like playing Grandmother's footsteps. I feel tricked, as if it's edging closer but I am never fast enough to catch it. I am straining my eyes to see it but it seems to happen when I blink. I make my eyes wide, holding the muscle tight until tears blur the green and my parents' voices sound far away. I hear Peg laugh. Peg and Brian came over while I was watching. Peg is drinking gin and talking about finding seals in Baghdad. There's a buzzing getting louder in my ears and the bud is swimming in green, it's spinning very slowly like a globe. Baghdad. In Germany we spun the globe, my globe with a bulb inside which lights up, and we took turns putting our fingers on the globe. I said we were going to the Pacific Ocean, my mother got Moscow but she said she didn't mean to put her finger so far north, it would be terrible for her cystitis so she tried again and this time she got Jordan but my father said no, it wouldn't be there because he doesn't speak Arabic, but he didn't know where either. I blink my eyes. Brian is talking about shooting ducks. More time has gone missing and now the top of the bud has split into five points. I am angry. The flower is cheating, it waits until I forget to watch and then it moves. "I can't see it move."

My father says, "But look, it's almost open."

"Yes, but I can't see it."

"Well, if we had a film camera and we filmed it and then we projected it fast, you'd see."

"Like on Walt Disney?"

"Yes."

"But then I should be able to see it now if I could look slowly enough. Or is it like when you draw pictures on the corners of the pages of a book and then you flip it and it looks like the people are running?"

"That's called animation," says my father.

Dave draws cartoons. But it's not the same. It's like nothing's happened and then it's happened but it must have done that all along, it must have been happening. If I could remember exactly how it looks now and then I'd wait a minute and then I'd remember again and wait half a minute and remember again and wait quarter of a minute and I'd keep on doing that till I wasn't waiting any time between remembering and seeing, then I'd see it happening. It would be like standing against the wall and putting a book on my head and making pencil marks and just making them all the time.

"Oh look, darling," says my mother, "you can almost see it move."

Almost. But it's true, the petals have spread so wide they are almost bending backwards and there is the smell. I didn't expect the moonflower to smell. It smells like meringues baking. No it doesn't. It smells like frangipani except it's thicker and not so sour behind the sweet and now it's all the smell there is. It's everywhere. I think I can see the flower breathing, the yellow in the middle, and the petals are longer than my fingers and white and thick. They shine. I want it to stop. Everybody. Stop. Stopped. Stop it. What will happen next? I am afraid. It happened too quickly and I didn't see.

My father is standing up, "Anyone for another drink?'"

It's over. But it can't just stop.

"Well, I shouldn't," says Peg. "I should totter home to bed, but what the heck, I'll drink to the flower. What do you think of that, me lovely?"

"What happens next?"

"Well now it dies. Me lovely dies." Peg's voice gets very sad. She waves her arm.

"And does that happen the same way?"

"Well, yes, but slower. What a funny question. She's a funny one isn't she?"

"It's time for you to go to bed. Look at Bill, he's sound asleep. It's midnight."

"I want to watch what happens next."

"You'll see in the morning. Go on up to bed now."

"Do what your mother says," says my father in the doorway with the glasses in his hands. "It'll be cool enough for you to sleep now."

I know I won't. I'll lie with my eyes open and imagine it and then in the morning if it looks like I think, I'll have seen.

Mrs. Welt

Mrs. Welt is talking about Gandhi. She is talking about America. What's happening now is history in the making. Civil Rights. Civil Disobedience. Dr. Martin Luther King Jr. Her hair stands up in perfect yellow circles except in front where it is dark and sticks to her forehead. The armpits of her turquoise sleeveless dress are sweaty too. She walks back and forth in front of the blackboard. All the time I've been in fourth grade I've never seen her in any other dress. Christopher says she must have five of them because she doesn't smell. She is from Texas but her name is German, you say it with a V. It means world. She is talking about sit-ins. I am remembering Sister Alice at the piano.

"What is so funny?" Her voice is flat and heavy like her footsteps.

"Nothing, Mrs. Welt."

"Who invented the tactic of nonviolent resistance?"

"Gandhi. But didn't other people do it too?"

"Yes," she stops walking back and forth, "I suppose the poor and the powerless of this earth have always resisted."

My heart gets big and heavy. I want my voice to be like hers. I want to smell under her arms. I want to sit on her knee.

Sister Alice

Sister Alice played piano at ballet at St. Corona's school where I was before this. I can see her in my head like I'm looking through a window into the room where it happened. Her mouth looks like she is holding pins. Her whole face reminds me of a pine tree. The one fan that stirs the air is down the other end of the room. Sweat runs down her cheeks and drips off her chin. Her foot pumps up and down as if she is driving a racing car. It is my second class. The teacher has made us stop and start again seven times. "Girls, girls," she cries each time but this time Sister Alice keeps on playing, her foot going up and down and the sweat spreading between her shoulder blades like dark wings.

The teacher, whose body looks like it comes apart at the joints and the waist like one of those blonde puppets on T.V., coughs. She coughs into her hand as if she is really coughing. I am praying now, Go Alice Go. Mrs. Hawkins raises her arms, "Girls, we will take those steps again." Sister Alice keeps on playing. She is playing something new, the notes chasing each other through the silence like flies in the jungle, like sunlight on a rock under a tree in the wind. Mrs. Hawkins drops her arms. She smiles. She smiles when she doesn't know what to do. If her voice had a smell it would smell of Parma violets. The girls edge back against the wall. Some hold onto the bar. Some are smiling. They want her to stop, they want things to go on like they're supposed to.

Mrs. Hawkins is tiptoeing toward the piano, she lifts her feet high off the ground, she grins at us like a pantomime villain. A girl giggles. Her name is April. Mrs. Hawkins is right by Sister Alice's shoulder now, she is poised to pounce, one hand curled in the air like a claw, like the Assyrian wolf who came down from the hills in *Peter and the Wolf.* Sister Alice doesn't pause, she doesn't flicker an eyelid. Mrs. Hawkins smiles. She stops being the wolf and heads for the door. She is only wearing her leotard.

Sister Alice's eyes are closed. Her fingers are gentle now as if the keys are wild animals she has taught to come to her. Her lips are soft. I don't know how she knows but right when Mrs. Hawkins appears in the doorway in her leotard with two nuns in their habits behind her, Sister Alice plays the last bars and then she sits, the notes hanging in the thick air, her hands in her lap, while the crepe shoes of the nuns squeak across the floor. No one else is allowed to wear shoes on this floor. When they stand on either side of her, she gets up, does an about face, and marches out between them. Her face is as smooth and pale as a sheet of paper. After she has gone I look at her shoes. They sit side by side by the door, pointing toward the piano. I want to leave her a note in one, "Be Brave, Your Ally," but one of the nuns comes and takes them away.

I never saw Sister Alice after that but I only stayed at St. Corona's for one term because I was bored and they wouldn't move me up a class. Now I'm a year younger than everyone but it doesn't matter. I want to know where Sister Alice went. After they took her away I still had to go to ballet but I wouldn't move when I was there and when they asked why, I wouldn't say but sometimes I laughed. I could hear the piano like sunlight and shadow. After a while they asked my parents to take me away.

Akueke

A dry wind is blowing, filling the house with sand from the north. Bill and I shape deserts on the window ledge.

I say, "It's from the Sahara."

"No it isn't."

"Is."

"Isn't."

"It's too hot to fight. Anyway I know because I'm older than you."

Christine walks by, her arms piled high with dirty clothes. Her body pushes at the seams of her crisp white dress and between her shoulders spreads a dark slick of sweat. Her broad cracked feet grip the tiled floor as she walks. She walks down the hall proud as a ship in sail. We play grandmother's footsteps until we are close behind her and then we pull up her dress. Dark coils between her legs. We run scared down the stairs. At the bottom I look back. She has set the laundry down. She is just standing. She isn't allowed to hit us. Bill giggles. I hate him.

I run outside, across the road, into the cemetery. I am dodging through the brush, sidestepping castles of dried red mud. They are everywhere. I don't want to. Christine has hair there too. I am giddy and out of breath. My mother is. Christine is. My name is Jake. I'm going to be an explorer. That's a secret. When you grow up. Woman. A fat smelly word. Woman. I got a doll for Christmas. I hid it. I played football with it then it was dirty and one arm broke off so I buried it. Christine won't tell. I didn't see. My name is Jake. Soldiers live in the buildings past the cemetery. Dust is stuck in my nose, in my mouth. In the cemetery are mud castles. I draw my foot back. I kick one. It falls apart. Inside are thousands of little rooms and termites scurrying, I see them each alone. It's a doll's house with the roof off. They swarm all up my leg. I stamp like a horse. They run up my dress. I run yelping into the house. "Christine. Christine." She pushes me into the bath and turns the water on full until there is a crust of insects floating dead. I am ashamed.

I am afraid. Christine tells me a story to make me brave. She says, "This is the story of my grandmother whose name is Akueke. My grandmother, my mother's mother, had a scar ran from her knee to her ankle. This is a scar she was dealt in fighting. This fighting took place when Akueke was young. It was a hungry year and she was gathering the yams with the other women. The British were coming next day to take away a large part of the harvest and the chief men were not stopping them because the British were giving the men the title of Warrant Chief. The British gave the men money more than cowrie shells but not to the women. As this was the case the chief women determined to hold a mikiri, a meeting of the women, and Akueke my grandmother was there. They met and they talked and they danced different dances, and one to be loyal, they spring forward, one arm high, and touch their hands. All through the mikiri should be a man bringing palm wine in a gourd in courtesy as is the custom but no man is coming and this is the way the men are behaving. So, as the women have decided, they take their machetes and the men's guns for hunting. They go together to the shrine of the old ones of the women and they cover each other with the medicine paste that is buried before the shrine. The paste is white so they are like ghosts now and fearful to behold.

"All the night they are saying to the men, 'Fight with us. You are Ibos too,' but the men are hiding in the huts. Shortly the British come and the women chase them away and then is high dancing. But the British return, many together, bringing guns. The women hide in the bush where there are large number of beasts, lions, jackals, et cetera and many are killed and wounded. Akueke, for example, her leg is torn in fighting, she lies in the sun for she cannot run. The British find her, they beat her to tell them where are the women hiding but she will not loose one word. They do many bad things to her. They leave her for the jackals to eat but she packs mud in her wounds and she crawls under a thorn tree. When it is morning she creeps to where the women hide which is nearby and they cry out to see so many bruises and especially the wound in her leg. She tells how she was loyal and they are glad with her and apply strong medicine so she is soon well.

"The women fight, also many women from other villages and some men, they fight for two years, they will not give up so finally the British must change their behavings. And in these troubles there is never a woman will tell the British where are the women though they are beaten into death but they will say, 'I am strong like Akueke, I am silent like Akueke.' This is the fighting where Akueke my grandmother received her scar. She told me this story when I was of your age as I should not be scared in the bush but brave like her."

Christine tells me now I must go back to the cemetery.

I go outside. I see that the lilies in the driveway have unfurled their orange trumpets and the blue lizards with poison in their heads crowd the walls of the servants' quarters. Where the cemetery begins I find a snakeskin wrinkled like one of my mother's stockings. It begins to rain.

I give the skin to Christine and I tell her about the flowers and the lizards.

"The dry season has come," she says. "Tonight everyone will drink palm wine and clap their hands." The rain is hammering at the roof the way it has every afternoon for six months. The air is thick as the smell of ripe bananas. I look at her. She smiles. "The lilies told me, " she says. "They only bloom when the Harmattan wind blows the dry season down from the desert. The lizards know too."

At seven the rain stops. The sun is like a mango when it sinks into the harbor. Drums beat in the villages across the lagoon, fires leap into the sudden night. It is dark in the house: the power is off again. Christine lights the hurricane lanterns, puffs of oily smoke hang in the air. I can see in her face she has gone far away to the secret place. I want to ask, why did the British kill the Ibos? I am silent. Sweat tickles my ribs and beads of water run diagonally down Christine's cheeks, following the lines of her tribe.

Blood Brothers

Dave is home from America. She gives me a special tie from Arizona. It is a leather lace with silver tips and a blue stone which is Lapis Lazuli.

"You wanna be blood brothers?" We are sitting on her bed after lunch.

"Sure," she says, "What do you have to do?"

"You cut your finger and I cut mine, then we swear an oath and we mix our blood."

"What kind of oath?"

"An oath for being brothers."

"O.K. I'll get Dad's razor."

"No, we should use something special. I sharpened my knife." I take it out of the leather sheath hanging at my belt and pass it to her, handle first. She takes it and drags the blade across her fingertip. Nothing happens. She pushes down with the point. Still nothing. "You try."

I look at my finger then jab the knife down. When I open my eyes there's no blood.

"Maybe we do have to use the razor," I say, so she goes and gets it and passes it to me. I take out the blade.

I hold my breath and slice across my finger. It doesn't hurt. I watch little balloons of red rise up in a line. They are like parachutes, a perfect landing at night over enemy lines. "Here," I say, passing her the blade but I can't stop watching. This is my blood. It looks foreign, like mushrooms. My finger is rimmed with yellow light and very far away.

"There," says Dave, waving her finger, "it's different when you do it on purpose."

"Yeah," I nod slowly. I am glad she is my friend.

"So what now?"

"We touch our fingers together and we swear our oath while the blood mixes."

I hold out my finger. She puts hers down on top of it. I see the blood squeeze out in between and I say, "I swear by our friendship"

"I swear by our friendship"

"To fight on your side,"

"To fight on your side,"

"To tell you the truth,"

"To tell you the truth,"

"To keep all your secrets,"

"To keep all your secrets,"

"Till death us do part."

"Till death us do part."

I look at my finger. The blood has gathered under the fingernail. "Teach me some more Judo," I say.

Bone

I lie in the grass with the crabs. It hasn't gone away. The party is almost over. Gabriel collects glasses. My shoulder hurts. When I think about it I don't know if it hurts. But just now I knew. I lean on it and the hurt burns down to my belly. I'm not making it up. I have to tell. Something gathers tight inside. Christine isn't here. It's her day off. I go in the house. Nobody sees. A man in glasses is saying goodbye. I stand with my feet crossed. He sees. My mother sees.

"Good God, darling, what are you doing still up? It's ten o'clock." I begin to cry. "You're all wet. What's the matter?"

"My shoulder hurts."

"Let me see," says the man. His robe is blue and white.

He lifts my T-shirt.

"Can you lift your arm?"

"Yes."

"This will hurt a little." He takes the shirt off very slowly, pauses when I wince. His glasses have thick tortoiseshell rims. He whistles. "Let's take her into the bathroom." Now I'm shivering in my stomach. I don't want to go in the bathroom. He turns to Gabriel, "Tell my driver I will be out shortly."

"You poor thing," says my mother, "How did you hurt yourself?"

I can't make the words come because I am crying again.

"Ssh," he says, "ssh." He puts his hand on my head and we walk upstairs. I sit on my mother's bed. She is standing up.

"Look at that bruise," she says. Now I want to scream. Somewhere far inside I can hear somebody screaming.

"What happened?" he says. His eyes are brown and kind. He wants to know.

"I was running down the hall and I tripped."

"This will hurt a little. Ready?"

I nod my head. He runs his finger down my collarbone. It feels as if his finger is reading me. It doesn't hurt very much.

"Fractured, I think," he says. "Do you have any bandages?"

My mother goes into the bathroom.

"When did you fall? A little while ago? Two hours? Three?" I nod. "Three hours ago," he says.

"Why on earth didn't you tell me?" says my mother.

I look at his hands. "I didn't want to interrupt."

"Don't be ridiculous. Of course I wouldn't have minded. You silly." She puts her hand on my head. I begin to cry again. I don't want to but I can't stop myself. "What a stroke of luck that you were still here, Dr. Ogunwe."

"Yes." He is frowning as he unrolls the bandage. I close my eyes. Tears keep leaking out. "Tomorrow you must take her to the hospital for an x-ray. Tonight give her a bag of ice to put on her shoulder when she sleeps."

I didn't make it up.

"It's probably a greenstick fracture. It will heal quickly. Children's bones are still soft, they don't snap like our old bones do."

“Speak for yourself, Dr. Ogunwe,” says my mother. She looks sideways at him. He smiles, but only a little. She goes and gets the ice. He sits on the edge of her bed, looking at me like he can see inside. I close my eyes. “Do you want to go to your room?” he says. I nod.

He waits outside in the corridor while my mother tucks me in. “Goodnight, darling, you’ll feel better soon.” She kisses me on my forehead. I can feel the tears begin to come again.

They go downstairs. I hear his car drive away. He is the last person to leave. I lie on my back. I can feel the ice melting.

City of Blood

Benin? They called it the City of Blood you know," says Peg. "It's the back of bloody beyond anyway. I can't say I envy you. What about the children?"

"It's only for three months. I'll come back to Lagos with them when school starts. Jack will finish up the last couple of weeks by himself."

"Knowing you, you'll come home loaded with treasures."

Leper

Something is on my bed. It isn't big but it is there. I slide my arm out from under the sheet and turn on the light. It is shiny black and armor plated. Its legs are square.

It keeps on climbing over me. It has a horn. The horn curves upward to a point. When it reaches the edge it walks down the metal leg of the bed. I think when it reaches the floor it will sound like a tank on a gravel road. It is as long as my longest finger. But it makes only a little ticking sound as it crosses the concrete floor.

Mr. Jones is patting my head. "Oh," he says," so you met one of our rhinoceros beetles, eh?" He has orange hair and a speckled face like a banana. Even the hairs on his legs are orange under his khaki shorts. He claps his hands. "Boy," he says.

I wipe my hair with my arm. His "boy" has wide brown eyes that look everywhere at once.

"Boy. More chop." He waves his hand at the empty pawpaw

skins in front of us. Boy brings fried eggs and tinned ham and takes away the skins.

"What are you chaps up to in the capital these days? Running around after the black boys now they have the whip hand?"

"Our relations with the federal government are pretty good now," says my father. He taps his cigarette once on the box and lights it. My mother makes a face but she keeps on eating.

"Reckon they can do without us now, don't they? I had some troublemakers among the workers but I sent them packing."

"It's important," says my father, knocking the ash off his cigarette, "you fellows stay on good terms with the government."

Mr. Jones yawns and as his hands reach the furthermost point of his stretch, he claps again. Red hairs stick out between the buttons of his shirt. I wonder if he is hairy all over. "More dash, that's all," he says, rubbing his finger and his thumb together as he brings his hand back to the glass of beer on the table. "Driver," he shouts. "Look," he says, "all they're doing is lining their pockets so they can keep mother and mother's brother's wife's sister and all her ten children in style. The different tribes squabble like children. Independence my arse. If it wasn't for us they'd still be living in the jungle in mud huts, hunting with bows and arrows. Now they've got guns, you mark my words, they'll be blowing each other's heads off before long."

"There is a whole new generation of educated Nigerians, nationalists, some very able young men coming into the government and the civil service. Colonialism is over, John." My father stubs out his cigarette hard.

My mother takes my brother and me to clean our teeth.

What a dreadful man," she says when my father comes into the bathroom.

“Darling, ssh.”

“Honestly, drinking in the morning. Granny always said if a man drank before sundown that was the end of him. Back then half the D.O.s ended up with D.T.s and picaninnies.”

“What’s a D.O.?” I ask.

“A district officer.”

“What are D.T.s?” says Bill.

“And picaninnies?” I say.

Our car is covered in orange dust. I draw lines on the hood like Christine’s lines. “How far is Benin from Enugu?”

“Far. Don’t get that laterite all over your clothes.”

“How far are we from Benin?”

“We’ll be there tonight if the ribbon cutting doesn’t go on too long.”

We are going to see the lepers after we see the rubber trees.

Touch it,” says Mr. Jones. It is sticky. “Roll some together. Now if you let it harden you’ll have a rubber ball.” Men cut Vs in the tree trunks with machetes. Others collect the latex that has gathered in buckets. The leaves of the trees are big and dark. The sap is white. The forest is silent except for the flies. The trees are in long orderly rows like pegs in a game, cribbage maybe. Bill has found a frog. He squats down to watch it. It is black with a thin blonde line outlining each limb. Its eyes swivel nervously. I can see its toes, fine as hair.

“Watch out for him,” says Mr. Jones. “That’s a spitting frog.” He talks about production. My mother waves the flies out of her eyes. “The new pesticide is excellent,” says Mr. Jones. “But the boys think it’s juju. Say it gives them stomach aches.”

It is getting hotter and hotter, and the air is sticky like the sap. It’s filling up my nose and mouth.

"Ow," says my brother. He jumps up, shaking his hand. "Ow."

"I warned you," says Mr. Jones.

Really, it's marvelous what you've done," says my mother.

"It's God's work," says the sister who has a knobby face and mousy brown hair poking out from under her headdress.

My mother smiles her sticky smile. Mr. Akumbe makes a speech. He is a big man in knee socks and spectacles like a giant boy scout.

"D.O.," I whisper to my brother.

"D.T.'s," he replies. We go on like that for a while. There is one dirt road leading up to a big gate set in the high wire fence surrounding the compound. Inside there are some low concrete buildings and two oil palm trees.

My father makes a speech, then he cuts a ribbon and people clap. Bill and I stand with my mother behind my father while somebody takes photographs. I am waiting for the lepers to come but they don't.

"Is it so they don't have to beg anymore?" I ask.

"Yes," says my mother.

"What is leprosy?"

"It's a terrible disease."

"Can I catch it?"

"No."

"Why not?"

"Oh for God's sake."

In the car the seat burns my legs. My mother hands us Ritz biscuits. We are going to the City of Blood.

"No wonder she married God, I bet nobody else would have her."

"She's done some wonderful work," says my father, "but I must say, she's no sight for sore eyes."

She is married to God. The lepers are God's children. I want to ask about this but Bill sticks his fingers in my ribs and says, "D.T.'s, Picaninnies D.T.'s, Picaninnies" very fast so I pinch him and I say "no nose no toes no nose no toes" over and over till he cries.

Ibeji

My mother is drinking gin with Peg. Dad is still in Benin. Tomorrow he has to go to the north to watch what is happening. I am a spy hanging on the rope ladder over the balcony. I have to watch my mother to make sure everything is all right. I have to keep an eye on things. My arms are aching. It's Christine's day off. I don't know where she went. She went to the secret place in her eyes. My mother's eyes are big and black today. A mosquito lands on my cheek. I can't move. She mustn't see me. Her eyes are looking at me. The mosquito tickles my cheek. It is sucking out my blood. Its body is swelling. I can see the blood traveling up the proboscis. Its compound eyes are glittering. I shift my hands on the rung. The ladder sways.

They don't see. They are looking at one of the statues from the dining room. Peg is holding it. It is one of the boy statues. She is pointing to his thing and laughing. She says, "Do you really think they are as big as this? I'd like to get my hands on one."

My mother giggles. "You are awful." She says it in a funny accent. Then she says in her normal voice, "But really, they are fascinating. I was reading about them last night. The Yoruba believe twins aren't human. They call them 'children of the monkey.' They're supposed to have supernatural powers so if a twin dies, which of course a lot of them do, they make a statue of it and then they wash it and feed it on special days."

"Just like children with their dolls. It's a bloody funny country. Don't mind me. You know I have the brain of a flea." Peg cackles and at the end of the cackle she snorts. Her black hair shakes up and down.

When it is still again my mother says, "They believe if you don't honor the dead twin he'll give the surviving one nightmares, maybe even kill him."

"Well all right but if they're statues of children why all this?" She waves at the boy's thing.

"I'll read you what the book says." She goes upstairs. Peg puts the statue down. She tips her glass all the way back. She holds it in front of her with both hands. It is empty except for one ice cube. Her eyelids are almost closed. Her face is red. Her mouth opens. "Gabriel," she says, "bring me another. One for Madam too."

My stomach is twisting but my mother is coming back onto the veranda so I stay still. She puts a book down on the table, a big book with pictures. She flips through it. "Here," she says.

Gabriel puts the glasses on the table. I know he saw me but he doesn't look at me. He is a Yoruba. His round face is pockmarked from smallpox. His eyes are red but his steward's jacket is white and stiff.

"Mother's ruin," says Peg, raising her new glass.

"Listen," says my mother. *"Blending infancy (in terms of height) with adulthood (in terms of sexual development) twin statuettes are a visual miracle, announcing the presence of the extraordinary."*

"Blimey. Must be a bloody American. Translate, please"

"They're children who can do it."

My mother is talking in a fake cockney accent.

"Fuckie, fuckie." Peg is snorting again. She is reaching for the statue.

I don't want them to touch him anymore. He will get angry. I climb down from the ladder. I stand by the bottle garden and look at them.

"Hello darling," says my mother. "Where did you come from? Look at that huge bite on your cheek. Say hello to Peg."

There aren't any words in my head.

"Well," says Peg, "I should be on my way."

I shake my head. I am looking at my mother's eyes.

"Silly girl," says Peg. "It's time for my din-dins."

She goes through a gap in the hedge. She lives next door. I don't see her go. I am looking at my mother. Her eyes are hungry. "I'm going down to the lagoon now," I say. The words come from far away. I pull myself away from her eyes. I run down the garden. I wish I could run on the water all the way to the sea.

Nigger

"Nigger," I say. I want to taste the word in my mouth.

Mrs. Welt's head jerks around. Mary is standing at the blackboard. She spelled *vegetable* right and now she is staring at it like she is going to eat each white chalky letter.

"Who said that?" I look at Mrs. Welt's belly. "Anna?"

Christopher giggles. "Both of you, go to the headmaster's office right now. I will not have that word used in my classroom." Her long Texas accent spins through the air like a lasso, her dress a perfect turquoise sky. The words hang for a moment over Christopher and me and then pull tight around us. "When you come back I expect you to apologize to Mary. Go." I've never heard her this angry. Tears prickle my eyes. I can feel my face is bright red, all my skin is hot as I walk toward the door.

We sit down on the bench outside Mr. Silver's office.

The red vinyl sticks to my legs. "My Dad says nigger whenever he's stuck in traffic," says Christopher. He has dark wavy hair and blue eyes and black eyelashes. He is the most beautiful boy in the class. Christopher is my favorite boy's name. All the boys say he is a sissy. One day Jonas came up to him and said, "Chrissie is a fairy, Chrissie is a fairy." I wanted to punch Jonas but Christopher wouldn't let me. He said it would be worse if a girl fought for him. If his father heard about that he would really beat him.

"Why does he beat you?"

"To make me a man."

"That's dumb."

Christopher shrugged the way he always does.

I think how Mr. Lee beats Jerry every Friday. He keeps a switch behind his golf bag in the living room. Jerry has to wait by the bag until his father calls him into his study. Jerry takes him the switch and Mr. Lee closes the sliding plastic curtain. I asked Jerry once why he didn't hide on Fridays. He said that would just make it worse, the waiting was the hardest part. Afterwards he always has tears in his eyes. Dave and Caroline and I play Chinese Checkers in the living room and we've never heard him yell.

I am getting nervous. "What do you think he'll say?"

Christopher shrugs. He brings his hands up from his elbows, he holds them palm up, empty. The door opens and the principal's secretary says, "Go on in now."

Mr. Silver has long bones and hair on his fingers and in his nose. "Tell me why you were sent to me?"

I take a deep breath. "I said 'nigger' and Christopher giggled when Mrs. Welt said 'Who said that?'" His face gets longer.

"Why did you say 'nigger'?"

"I don't know sir."

"What does 'nigger' mean?"

"It means a black person." I wish he would close his door. I know Miss Austen can hear every word and she is black too.

"It's a word white people use to make themselves feel better than black people. That's not what this school is about. In this school we are equals. The color of somebody's skin does not make them better or worse than you. Whether somebody is English or American or Nigerian or whatever does not make any difference. We are equals." His eyes go sideways to his watch. "Equals," he says, and he smiles and his whole face wrinkles like a turtle.

Why are all the teachers white? Why aren't there any white beggars except lepers who aren't really white? Why are servants black? I want to ask him but I don't.

When we turn the corner of the corridor, Christopher says, "What a joke. Look, we missed almost the whole class."

I don't say anything. In the classroom I go up to Mary. She sits near the door. "I'm sorry, Mary," I say. She just looks at me, a flat nothing look. "I'm sorry I said that. I just was jealous because you spelled vegetable right and won." I can't make her eyes look any different. Then I see my fist going into her stomach. I just keep staring at her eyes and then I walk away. I didn't punch her.

"Christopher," says Mrs. Welt.

"'Pologise, Mary," he says.

Trips

We were starving. Bill was whining because he ran out of ketchup, when out of nowhere came this man in a loincloth carrying a bow and arrow. He was walking along the side of the road. When he saw us he went away. When he came back we were still there. We were lost. He brought a basket of red fruit like little peppers. He said, 'Cashew.' My father opened the trunk and gave him five empty whisky bottles and three empty ketchup bottles. When the man smiled his teeth were sharpened to points. Bill said he was a cannibal but I didn't think so. He didn't have any hair on his legs."

"What's that got to do with him being a cannibal?"

"Nothing. He poured the fruit into a towel and then my father took out his camera. He waved it towards the man and the man smiled but when he pointed it at the man, he put his hand in front of his face and then he disappeared."

"What do you mean, he disappeared?"

"He wasn't there anymore."

"Where did he go?"

"I don't know."

"Was it jungle?"

"No, it was bush."

"You're weird."

"It's not me that's weird. I just see weird things."

"People don't just disappear."

I shrug. "My father says some people believe that if you take a photograph of them you steal their spirit."

"That's dumb."

Dave bends down to retie the shoelaces on her high-top sneakers. Her face is hidden behind her knee. She says, "I wish my family went on trips."

"You did, in Arizona."

"Here, in Nigeria."

"Maybe you could come with us on one."

"Yeah?" she says. She keeps on tying her laces into double knots.

Mom," I say, when she's finished taking the bones out of her fish, "the next time we go on a trip can we maybe take Helen along too?"

"No darling we really can't. And don't talk in that dreadful American accent."

I forgot. Usually I don't forget.

"Why can't we?" I wait. I can feel my face getting red.

"The Lees wouldn't like it."

"But what if Helen asked them and they said yes?"

"They're our family trips. They're just for us."

"I want Jerry to come too," says Bill. He has ketchup on his chin.

"But why?"

"Don't argue with your mother," says my father.

"I don't get it," I say to my fish.

"What did you say?" says my father. I keep looking at the fish's white eyes. "Look at me when I'm talking to you." I force my eyes up. "Now, what did you say?"

"I said I don't get it."

"Speak English," says my father.

"I told you we should never have taken her out of St. Corona's," my mother says.

I look at my plate very hard.

"Let's drop the subject shall we?" says my father.

I can feel his eyes on my neck.

"Yes," I say.

"There wouldn't be room in the car anyway," he says.

The next day Dave says, "I asked Mom and Dad and they said maybe I could. Go on a trip with you."

"Dad said there wouldn't be room in the car." I look at her. "I'm sorry."

"Is that true?"

"I guess. Bill said he wanted Jerry to come too."

"But you asked first."

"I know. It's not fair."

We don't say anything. Then Dave says, "When we're older we can go away to sea and go wherever we want."

"To the Amazon."

"To the Galapagos."

"To Greenland."

"To Tierra del Fuego."

Dave makes the secret sign and I make it back. I want her to see the things I see.

Killings

"Make that two gin and limes and a lime juice, Gabriel, please." I sound like my mother.

My father sets his briefcase down beside the long blue chair. He pulls up the back so it is upright. He sits down and stretches out his legs. His feet stick out over the end.

"Darling, you look exhausted."

He shakes his head. "There's been another massacre in the north. That's over six thousand dead already, almost all Ibos." There are big rings of sweat under his arms. "They're panicking now. Hundreds of thousands are leaving. It's chaos." He passes my mother the *West African Chronicle*. On the front page is a fuzzy grey photo: a long snake of Mammy Wagons and motorcycles and bicycles and carts. Everything looks dusty.

"Where are they going?" I ask.

"Mostly back home to the Eastern Region. Some will come to Lagos."

"As if there aren't enough people here already," says my

mother. "How dreadful. These poor people. To lose their homes just like that. Can you imagine?"

"The government's sending in more troops. The trouble is the police force in the north is mostly Hausa and there's a lot of resentment against the Ibos. And if the blasted Ibos really try to secede." He shakes his head.

"What does it mean, to secede?"

"To call themselves another country."

I open my mouth but my mother says, "Darling, really, you look exhausted."

"I am. It was damned hot today." He finishes his drink and gets up. "I think I'll have a shower before dinner."

When Daniel brings in the filet of sole he looks taller and more dangerous. I wonder if secretly he hates Christine. Mostly he doesn't talk to anyone. He sits in the kitchen and reads the newspapers when my father has finished with them.

"What did the Ibos do wrong?" I ask.

"They've done too well is what it boils down to. They're a shrewd and cunning lot on the whole. They've adapted to the modern world better than most so they've made a lot of headway in business and industry and in the army and the civil service too and the others don't like it. Which isn't surprising because, like every other group in the damned country, when they're in positions of power they favor their own people."

"At least," my mother says, "the British have always been known for our fairness. I know there are people who wish we were still running the country."

Daniel brings in meringues with whipped cream. They look like drifts of snow. When I bite into one it is crispy outside and chewy inside.

"Mmmm," says my brother.

"I'm afraid," my father says, "this is just the beginning. I'm afraid there's going to be a blood bath."

Mamba

I am wearing my red string T-shirt and my jeans. I look at where the band at the end of the sleeve circles my biceps. The shadows of the bamboo make lines across my forearm like Christine's lines. I bend my elbow and clench my fist and watch the muscle bulge. My muscle moves sideways like a hermit crab when I twist my wrist and my T-shirt is red like the canna lilies. All the talk stops in my head. I look up into two black eyes, black all the way back inside and like a tunnel leading from me into them and I am sucking out of me down that tunnel out of me. I've gone black inside and far away. I don't end anywhere. Black like in between the stars and green between and now inside my chest there are these words: "Don't move."

I remember my feet. They're stuck to the ground. The words are in my chest. I'm in the tunnel and then black goes blacker and washes away in grey. I see flat grey metal and brown and a brown hand and hanging in the air a green and yellow and brown, a snake. Jeremiah with his machete killed the snake. I know the head is on the ground. I look and it is right near my sandal. I hold tight. If the eyes are black I'm O.K. They're grey. Where did the black go? I want to throw up. Jeremiah takes my hand. My hand is brown too.

"Mamba," he says. "Green mamba is a deadly snake. It is good you did not move."

He straightens up, hooks the body of the snake off the bamboo, carries it away on the blade of his machete, careful not to touch. The head is still lying at my feet. I could be dead now.

Woman

Dave never tells me stories, she makes cartoons instead. All the people have square jaws. The boys have slicked back hair and the girls have ponytails. She gave me a cartoon of my father. I keep it in my marine chest. First he is holding a golf club, ready to swing. He is looking straight ahead. Then he is running and his knee is very sharp and almost up to his chin, the other leg points straight out behind him toward the swarm of bees which chase him like a long black cloud. Then he is lying in a ditch of water with only his feet sticking up and the cloud is passing over him and there is a frog sitting on a log with its mouth open. Then there is a big picture of the frog with its mouth so wide it looks like it is laughing. The frog has spots on its back and if you look close the spots are really bees.

She hands me the one she just made. There is a boy with a stick sticking out in front of his jeans. He is whistling. In the next frame there is a girl. Her eyes are big and round and her eyebrows look like question marks. Her mouth is an O and in between her legs is another O. Then there is a car. Then the boy and the girl are standing opposite each other. The little lines behind their legs say they are walking towards each other. Then the boy's stick is in the girl's O. Where the stick sticks through the O it is drawn in dots. The girl's feet don't touch the ground anymore and the boy isn't whistling.

I look at it for a long time. "Where does it go?" My cheeks feel so big and red I can see them out of the bottom of my eyes. I have to know. My stomach hurts.

"It goes inside the girl," says Dave.

"But where?" I want to cry. "There isn't room."

Dave goes in her closet and puts her hand in one of her sneakers. She brings out a piece of paper which she unfolds and spreads on her knee. There, against a blue background, is a woman, all white. She is cut in half. She has long pointy fingernails. It is a diagram. She is pushing a small stick up a gap which leads to something that looks like a catcher's mitt only it has more fingers. It looks like something that grows on the bottom of the ocean.

"Where did you get this?"

"The trash. I found something else in the trash too. It's a secret."

I look at her. "We're brothers, remember."

She takes this piece of paper out of her other sneaker. It is bigger and shinier. She starts to unfold it. One side is jagged like it was torn out of a book. First I see the beach and then I see shoes. They are black and shiny with pointy toes and long thin heels which sink down in the sand. Then we go up her legs which are long, too, and far apart. Dave stops. She goes to the door and listens then she unfolds it another time and where her legs meet there is hair, it is yellow and glinty except in the middle where something pinkish brown sticks down like a tongue.

"That's her pussy," says Dave.

"I know," I say because I need to hear my voice sound big and strong but it doesn't and then I say, "It's yellow," which doesn't make any sense to me either.

Dave keeps going. The woman has sharp red fingernails. She holds her waist in and her nails point down like little neon lights. I want to say stop but then there is her bosom.

"Tits," says Dave.

They are like balloons full of water with the knots sticking out. Her arms stick out from her body so you can see the beach and the sea and on the right side there is a palm tree, only I can't see the top of it yet. Then there is the rest of the tree and her neck is long like the tree. It goes up and up to her chin which is tipped back. Right by her neck the paper is torn.

"Who is it?" I say to Dave.

"I don't know. It's just someone in a magazine."

The woman's mouth is huge and red and shining. It is an O too, only I can see the tip of her tongue in the corner of her mouth. It is curled around like a snake's tail and her teeth are very big and white. I am afraid to see her eyes, I know they will be hard and black but they aren't, they are half covered with eyelids, and her eyelashes are so long it is like she is looking through tall grass at me. I can see the wind in her hair and the sky is blue. Dave whistles.

I take the piece of paper and hold it in front of me. The way she is standing is weird. It is like she is pinned out on a board, like the seahorse in Peg's house. "I don't get it."

"You're not supposed to get it dummy."

"What's it for?"

"It's for men to look at. Sailors do it all the time."

"Oh."

"That's what they do when it's too dark to fish."

Dave knows she knows something I don't. I don't care. My head feels crowded. I keep thinking how she couldn't go anywhere in the sand with those shoes. It is a thought which keeps the other thoughts back.

"You wanna take it?"

"What?"

"Her, dummy."

"Why?"

"You could put it in your marine chest with the equipment."

"Why don't you keep it?"

"Because it's better in your chest. You can lock it."

I know Dave's mom snoops a lot. "O.K."

"Take the other picture too."

"No, throw that in the trash." I fold her up and put her in my pocket. When I get home I'll put her inside my flashlight wrapped around the batteries.

War

"Well, they've done it," my father says. He folds the paper and puts it down on the table.

"More tea, darling? Done what?"

"Seceded. As of today the Eastern Region wishes to be known as the Republic of Biafra."

He pinches the skin in between his eyebrows. My mother is tipping the teapot but no tea comes out of the spout.

"It means war. As sure as eggs is eggs there's going to be a civil war. It's just a matter of time."

I read the date on the paper upside down: 30th May, 1967.

"Gabriel," my mother says.

Soldiers

It's bedtime. Christine is by the window. She's reaching to draw the curtains when the lights go out. In the silence after the air conditioner stops whirring we hear shouting from the barracks on the other side of the cemetery. The shouting gets louder. Soldiers are coming down the road. They are chanting something. They are chanting, "We want Christine the Ibo. Give us Christine the Ibo." It is dark in the house but by the light of their torches we see them, Christine and my mother and my brother and I standing in the upstairs hallway. In their hands are long leather whips. They tilt their heads to drink, faces shining with sweat, the green glint of bottles passing hand to hand, they are twenty or more. Christine hides in the closet in my parents' room. The soldiers are talking. From the dark inside the house I hear her voice, muffled.

> Our Father which art in heaven
> Debe m ndu Ji rue nne Omumu bea
> Omumu bea

The claws of the land crabs click on the veranda and the soldiers' boots clatter gravel in the driveway. They are chanting slowly now. "Christine the Ibo. Christine the Ibo." The phone doesn't work. The soldiers edge closer. They crack their whips. The doors are locked. It is the house of white people.

Ji rue nne Omumu bea

I hear it first. The noise of jeeps on the road. It grows into a roar. I see them now, their headlights catching the graves and termite castles of the cemetery. The military police take the men away. Christine hides long after they have gone.

Brownies

It is ninety-five degrees and the humidity is ninety-eight percent. We are tying half-hitches and bowlines and reef knots in Mrs. Samuels's clothesline. I am a Brownie. At night I read the book. There are drawings of girls in mountains and of pieces of celery and carrots. Celery and carrots are perfect for a hiker's lunchbox. They are nutritious and they quench your thirst. I learn what to do if my companion is bitten by a rattlesnake and that moss grows on the north side of trees and rocks. I learn how to find north using the sun and a wristwatch.

Mrs. Samuels's backyard is narrow. It has high wire fencing on either side and the fence is hidden by morning-glory vines. After we have tied knots we make a fire and we toast marshmallows and put them on graham crackers with milk chocolate. We hold them in the flames again so the chocolate bubbles and darkens. The smell of it lines the roof of my mouth. Joseph, her son, kneels on the sofa in her living room and watches us through the window. When her husband comes home he slams the car door then he slams the front door. She doesn't look up. We sit around the fire and eat the s'mores and sing songs about the Brownie way of life from the back of the book. There are five of us and Mrs. Samuels. Mrs. Samuels leads the singing. She has a narrow face with wide apart red-brown eyes and her mouth twitches but if you were blind and you heard her singing you would think she was five-foot-ten and muscled and had a wide blonde freckled face. She was in the Brownies when she was a girl.

Today she is wearing sunglasses. She never did before. Every few minutes she touches her left cheek with her fingertips. Her wrists are so thin they look like sticks you could break to build a fire. I edge around the circle until I can see down the side of her glasses. She has a black eye. It is swollen shut. "Mrs. Samuels," I say, "What happened to your eye?"

"I stepped on a rake," she says. She says it quick. She says, "Never leave a rake lying on the ground."

She tells us how when she was in the Brownies they went camping in New Jersey and she caught a fish in the river and cooked it over a fire she made herself. She says it was the best feeling in the whole world. It was like being a pioneer. She lived in the Bronx when she was growing up. In the book it talks about lying out at night looking at the stars. I want to ask about her eye again. I say, "When are we going camping?"

Rebecca says, "Dummy, you only go camping in America."

I say, "People go camping in England all the time." I think about how if we do go camping I won't be able to pledge allegiance to the flag when we run it up in the morning.

Mrs. Samuels says, "It's too hot to go camping in Africa and there are too many wild animals."

I know it was her husband who hit her eye. I can see the black hair on his wrist and his gold watch. I don't remember ever having looked at him but I know how his wrist looks and I know it was him. I want Mrs. Samuels to catch fish again but she looks too thin. I look at her wrists again. I could break them over my knee. On her forehead the veins stick out blue, they look wet and cold like a fish. I think of her lying on a rock, gasping for air. Her husband is standing over her looking at his hands as if they don't belong to him. I want to stop thinking this thought. I look at the morning glory flowers, how blue they are, how there isn't anything there except color, how they are blue in the shape of a flower. She is a grown-up and she gets hit. It is a secret.

When we are waiting for our mothers to pick us up I go up behind Rebecca and I say very quietly, "There's a scorpion on your sock."

She looks down and then she says, "I don't believe you."

"No really," I say, "it's on the back. It's climbing up. Hold still." She squeals. I say, "What would you do if you got bitten by a rattlesnake? They have them in America," and I walk away.

In bed I read the last chapter of the book. It is about getting up early in the morning and doing the chores before Mother gets up. In the picture the girl has on a little elf hat and she is peeking out from behind a door while her mother stands in the kitchen with her hands in the air. There are little shine marks like tufts of grass on the stove and the kettle and the windows.

Spartan boys ran ten miles a day and lived in barracks away from their parents. I would have been a boy in Sparta.

Fever

"Malaria, I'm afraid," says the doctor. I am cold. Blankets score my skin. I am hot. I shiver. The rain clatters in my skull. It draws a curtain of beads across the window. The curtain is moving. My skin is grey with ice. The curtain of water is green as a mamba, its black-bead eye holding mine. Christine. My tongue sticks to the roof of my mouth. Christine is gone in a mammy wagon, she wears a colored headcloth, orange and blue. She is going to find her family in the bush where the war is. The soldiers raped and flogged another Ibo woman to death. Christine waves from the lorry. I cry when we get home. Her white dress is on the chest in the hallway. Quinine is bitter. Her dress is ironed and folded. The fever comes and goes. My father is home from the front. He was an observer. He flew up and down. He flew up and down with Prince Richard. Every night the power is out. Voices. My father's. The war will be over soon. The Biafrans can't last. They're surrounded. There's no food or fuel left. Days slide into each other. I get up, I walk down the stairs, step by step, a long way between each one. I am watching

Mission Impossible. My father is home from the embassy. He tells my mother, "I got a letter from Christine today. God knows how it got through. She wants a diplomatic pass. Her village is gone. She couldn't find any of her family." Christine is coming back. "She'll never make it. Don't tell the children." There are pictures of Biafra in the magazines beside the T.V. Christine is coming back. The fever returns. I smell my mother, powdery, too sweet, she shakes a silver stem. "Don't bite it by mistake. Leave it in until I come back." Dad is going back to the war. Christine stands in a deserted village. There are no women pounding cassava. The yam patch is a charred square. She is wearing her white dress. She is in the bush. A child stands with a tight round belly, crying. That's a photograph. A black march of ants crosses a heap of limbs rotting in the sun. My mother props the thermometer in a glass by my bed.

"When is Christine coming back?"

"I've told you a hundred times, I don't know. It'll be a miracle if she got the pass, let alone the money. We'll just have to wait and see."

I know from her voice she doesn't believe Christine will come. I turn my face to the wall. In a dream I see Christine. She stands in a triangle where three paths meet. Her feet are red with mud. There are no people, only the chatter of birds high in a breadfruit tree. The tree is one hundred feet tall. At the base of the tree is a snake coiled in fat loops around a breadfruit. Christine squats and speaks to the snake. It slides away. She builds a small fire and roasts the fruit. When she has eaten she walks on, choosing the wider track. I cannot see her eyes. I know she is coming.

Twin

Dave and I are sitting in the pawpaw tree in her backyard. I can reach out and touch an almost ripe pawpaw. Its skin is green but it is soft.

"Papaya," says Dave, "not pawpaw."

I say, "I'm going to tell you something that happened and it's a secret. " She just sits there in her jeans and her white T-shirt with the creases still in it. She's too cool to ask and maybe she doesn't believe me because a lot of things happen to me that don't happen to other people. "Promise not to tell anyone?" She nods. Jenny is in her room. She's playing a record by the Monkees. I can see her dancing around in her bra and brushing her hair. She's got a date tonight. She won't even say hello to us. Her bra is white with a rose in the middle. "I never told anybody this. I had a twin too but he died."

"Yeah? Why did he die?'"

"Because I ate too much and he didn't get enough."

"What was his name?"

"I don't know. He died before he got a name."

“Who told you.”

I shrug. Suddenly I’m scared. I don’t know.

“Did you see him when he died?”

I nod.

“What did he look like?”

“He was tiny and shriveled with a huge belly. Nobody listened when he cried so he ate himself up. That’s what happens when somebody starves to death.”

Dave looks at me. I can’t see inside her eyes. I say, “Have you ever seen a dead person?”

“Yes.”

“Where?”

“On T.V.”

“I mean a real one.”

“My Dad says there were lots of dead people in Korea and he and Mom are lucky to be alive in America.”

I nod. I think about Mrs. Lee’s skin moving over the bones in her face like thin cotton. Then I see Mr. Lee on the golf course in plaid Bermuda shorts, his thigh, thick and smooth and golden, stretching the material tight as he prepares to swing.

Jenny opens the back door. She looks as if all of her has been ironed. Dave wolf whistles. Jenny says, “Tell Mom I’ll be home at ten.”

Island

With my knife I carve pegs and at low tide I drive them deep in the sand, anchoring the low wall I have woven from palm fronds. I watch the moon. When the tide has gone out again I gather the fish from my trap. Their night bodies are silver and green. Some I lay on racks over a smoky fire, some I wrap in clay and roast in the embers. On my island there is a spring and where the spring flows from the ground there is red clay. I cook in clay, I make masks I hang from trees so spirits will guard me. I whistle. This is where I was born. In clear water I dive for oysters, the knife between my teeth. I slide the blade into the muscle, watch the shell open. It is soft on my tongue, the sea taste of oyster. Whatever pearls I find, I give to the spirits. Some are black, some are white, the pearls that shine in their faces. I know the ways of sea cucumbers, how they inch their brown bodies along the rocky ledges of the bay. In the heat of the day I drink green coconut milk; turtles bury their eggs on my beach. My heart is big for my chest. I sing. I hide my fire when ships pass on the horizon.

When I was beginning Grandmother Turtle rode me on her back. Dolphin swam beside me. They taught me to swim. They said, "The blood in your body, it is water. Water surrounds you. The sea in your body speaks with the tides." I floated. I listened to the sea's heart. At last Dolphin said, "Come and play," and I swam out of the dark. I swam like a squid, pulsing in the waters.

When the bird came I didn't know. I rode in the sky on its creaking wings. I was given a name sharp on their tongues, the big ones. I was cunning and small. I took what I needed. I hid my strength. I was a baby, always hungry. I cried. My mother smiled. Her hands were angry. My father stood tall but he was afraid. I belonged to them.

One day they left me at the water's edge to play. I heard the dolphins calling. Water answered water. I swam. Like any fish at night I shone in the dark. But the dolphins were sad for me. I had grown legs and arms. They brought me to my island. At sunset they play for me. When I eat I thank the sea.

Return

Christine arrives at our back door the same day the rains end. She is thin, her clothes muddy and torn. I wouldn't have recognized her. She says, "You've grown," and smiles. But her eyes are tired and like she doesn't look into the secret place anymore. She goes to wash and sleep. The next day she is wearing her white dress. It hangs from her body in folds. Alongside the beauty lines are new lines scored deep in her face. I watch her doing the laundry, squatted on the ground, slapping and turning the wet cloth on the board. Beads of water zigzag down her face. I touch her cheek with my finger. She pushes me away.

Cycle II

⁂

The English Ibeji

1965–1968

Christmas

I leave my parents sleeping to run across the sand, my toes curled against the heat. I squat within reach of the longest waves, the hiss of water reaching up between my legs, drawing back, leaving a damp pad of sand in my bikini bottoms. Sometimes a wave reaches up to my belly, swirls around me, sucking the sand from under my feet. It is part of my discipline not to run from these. I watch a man stand in his dugout, one long oar held loosely, waiting. The sun is low in the sky so the man's shadow lies in front of him on the water and when at last the wave he waits for comes, it's as if he rushes into his own shadow to capture it before the sea can steal it from him. The dugout comes like the dark fin of a fish lifted higher and higher as the wave swells until the sea spits it out onto land and the children run into the water, seizing the bow, dragging it out of reach of the breakers.

I am shy of this man and his children gathered around the boat but I want to see in, to see the squirming silver, green, and blue, the sharp bodies of barracudas with their thin white teeth, snappers, mullet. I watch their eyes cloud. This time there is a shark with its gritty body and sideways eyes, the slit of its mouth pursed and lipless. Its head is weird, oblong. "It's a hammerhead shark," I say. The children are already scooping the fish into buckets. When the canoe is empty the oldest boy, whose name is Emmanuel, washes it out with bucket after bucket of sea water. I am afraid for his elbows and knees, the bones so bare they are waiting to break. Afterwards he turns the canoe over. He spreads the nets across it and checks them for tears.

I walk along the beach, thinking about Granny. I walk where the sand is damp and cool. When we go home on leave we will go to the Isle of Man where she lives. I can see her, bony and hollow-flanked like her old cat, Tiger, who is dead now. Granny wasn't always like that. I can see her in her pith helmet, standing in front of the high wire fence of the compound, her belly bulging in her white dress. Her dark hair makes her face whiter. Everything except her hair looks white, even the trees glare like ghosts. She is waiting for the ice boat, which will bring ice and tinned food and letters, which will take the letter she has written asking for a passage to England. My mother says it was touch and go whether Granny would reach Liverpool in time for my mother to be English. "What would you have been if you had been born on the Gold Coast?" I asked. She handed me the bottle of Ambre Solaire and asked me to rub it in between her shoulders. I imagined my hands at the ends of long rubber sticks, so long they didn't belong to me. "Would you have been an African if you hadn't been born in Liverpool?" I was wondering if I would have been African too and if that meant she would have been black and if I would have been too even if she married my father anyway, like Anthony, whose mother was white but he was still black. She said, "Perhaps, but probably something could have been worked out." She put her cheek on her arm and closed her eyes.

She doesn't look anything like Granny though she has black hair. Granny's face is long like a horse where my mother's is round. Granny's name is Anna and my mother's name is Anna and my name is Anna. I have brown hair like my father's. Granny told me at night she used to hear the lions padding around the fence and the hyenas howling. She lay in bed and thought, "This is an adventure." She told me this when we visited her before we ever came to Nigeria and it was just a name I said in bed at night, Nigeria, Nigeria, Nigeria. She showed me her methylated spirits cooker which packs in a container no bigger than a biscuit tin. On the inside of the lid are instructions. They are too blackened with smoke to read. She insisted on taking the tin with her to Africa for expeditions though my grandfather who died in the war laughed at her.

Walking down the beach I smell methylated spirits, I see the shimmer that rose from the cooker making everything wavy. Everything is shining. A huge glittering white boat is floating in the heat. The ice boat. I look down at the sand. The branch of a tree sparkles like frost against the white sand. I break off a needle. It is crusted with tiny square crystals of salt. It smells of turpentine, it smells of mountains and dark green. I drag it back down the beach. My father and brother lie under the umbrella. The umbrella is blue and white. My mother lies in the sun. She lies face up. She isn't wearing her bikini top. I don't look at anyone. I drag the branch right into the shade.

"Is it a Christmas tree? Darling, how clever of you. What a find."

She puts on her top. She comes into the shade. We sit in the circle of shade. Outside the sand gets whiter and whiter. They break needles and the shade smells of pine. We sit in a circle. It is Christmas day, nineteen hundred and sixty five.

Trader

Gabriel says, "Madam, the trader is here."

He says that every Friday. My mother goes outside. The trader is a thin man in khaki shorts with a white rag wound around his head. His eyes are long and thin too. With a flick of his toes he pulls out the kickstand of his bicycle. He carries the burlap sack from the bicycle to the shade of the front porch. Before he opens it he says, "Madam, I have one, two thing very special, very old. The other ladies, they do not know. You have a knowing eye. I will show you what I have."

He brings out the things one by one, unwrapping the newspaper from each and pausing. My mother watches silently as he lays out ashtrays of Kano silver, wooden masks with round eyes, small bronze lions. Then he pauses a second longer and with a sigh unwraps the special thing. This Friday it is a pair of wooden figures. As my mother reaches for them he says, "These are very very old, Madam" and stands them side by side. Surrounded by the ashtrays and masks, they stare straight ahead with heavy lidded eyes. One is a woman. Her breasts hang down to her belly button. The other has a huge thing which sticks out. They are dusted with blue powder which clings to the dark wood as if it is skin. Their legs are squat and bowed, they aren't even a foot tall but they are heavy, they are heavy with themselves. There is something else I can feel but I can't say about them.

My mother wants them. The trader knows this. She asks him to show her the rest of his goods and she watches until he has unwrapped the last bundle, then she points to the figures. "These are Yoruba?" She is using her African voice. It isn't pidgin but it isn't ordinary English. She speaks slowly, the words stiff and separate like Lego bricks. "From what region do they come?"

"This I do not know. I bought them from another trader. I paid a high price because I knew Madam would be interested."

"How much you want for them?"

"Fifty pounds, Madam"

"Oh no, John, what you think I am an American? I can give you twenty-five pounds."

His face becomes so long it seems to hang down from his forehead like a rag as he reaches for the figures to wrap them in newspaper. "Madam, I myself paid forty pounds."

"I will give you thirty pounds."

"Madam, Madam."

When my father comes home she says, "Darling, look what I got from John today, a pair of Ibejis, aren't they marvelous?" He holds them in his long hands and frowns. "They're a real find, listen to what the book says." She opens it to where the marker is.

"How much did you pay for them?"

"Listen. This is the explorer Richard Lander in 1830: *Many women with little wooden figures on their heads passed in the course of the morning, mothers who having lost a child, carry imitations of them about their persons for an indefinite time as a symbol of mourning.*

None could be induced to part with these affectionate little memorials. Whenever the mother stopped to take refreshment, a small part of their food was inevitably presented to the lips of these inanimate memorials."

"How much were they?"

"Twenty-five pounds."

"Anna love, we just don't have that kind of money to throw around."

"Any museum would give their eye teeth to get their hands on these." He doesn't reply. "We'll eat mince for a week sweetheart."

"How are we going to get them out of the country? The government doesn't allow the export of antiquities, you know."

"Just look at them darling, aren't they marvelous?"

"They are very fine," he says. He bends down to look at the pair squatting on the long glass coffee table between the two Benin bronze leopards. They are standing side by side. They don't look at him. They were sold. They don't want him to touch them. The word I couldn't find for them is angry.

Ma

The pink and wrinklies are taking us out for dinner. My grandmother is putting her face on. She does it every morning but today she's doing it twice. First she shows me her feet. The toes are crooked and grey and they all grow together to a point. "Look at this, young Anna," she says. "When I was a girl I wore winkle pickers and all I thought about was boys."

"What are winkle pickers?"

"Stilettos," she says. "Shoes with pointed toes and thin high heels. They were all the rage."

Stiletto, I say in my mind. The word is thin and dark and dangerous. Stiletto.

"The young men couldn't keep their eyes off me," she says, rubbing her toes. "I was quite a looker. After I married George he wouldn't let me out of his sight, he was so jealous."

She's smiling. I can see my grandfather's pale blue eyes following her round and round the room not even stopping to look down at his beer. I wriggle my toes. "I'm not going to get married," I say.

She smiles. "Don't be silly, dear. Don't let your old grandmother put you off with her stories. Young women these days don't wear winkle pickers, they're more sensible than we were."

"No," I say, "I'm not going to get married."

"Before I can say Jack Robinson, you'll have some handsome young man courting you and then, before you know it, you'll be married. You're a pretty girl, young Anna Gwyneth, those lovely big eyes and curly hair. Don't you worry, the boys'll be lining up."

She is looking in the mirror now. She paints red dots on her cheeks and then she rubs them out. She draws lines along her eyes. She is casting a spell over me. In my head I say over and over, I'm Jake, I'm Jake, I'm Jake.

What does she look like before she puts her face on?"

Christine chuckles and looks at me, shaking her head. Ma acts like Christine's not there except sometimes she wrinkles her nose and gives an order as if she is very far away. Christine's feet slap the floor as she obeys.

"Christine, I don't have to get married, do I?"

"Girl," she says, "when your time is ready you will be wanting a husband. I too was like you. I wanted to stay in my father's house. When the fruit is ripe it fall from the tree. How is a woman without children?" In her eyes is the far away. I don't say anything.

Drunk

Wasipichu masipichu mau mau niggers rose up killed the whites rose in the dark and by treachery killed them they rose in the dark killed women and children they rose they rose black rose in the dark gotta keep an eye on the natives smile and smile and be smile in your face whass going in their heads smiling happy go lucky not a care at night in the dark in the dark niggers."

The wind from the lagoon carries his voice. Donald is hitting the casuarina tree with the flat of his hand. He stumbles. Gabriel in his white uniform is holding him up. Donald's pale blue and white seersucker pants shine against the lagoon. His arm is around Gabriel's neck.

"I'm dreadfully sorry," says my mother's voice. "Really, he's too awful."

I lean my head over the railing of the balcony. The police commissioner is very tall and still. He is wearing a grey and white tie-dyed robe.

"Drunkeness," he says, "is most certainly a problem among the foreign corps. *In vino veritas* perhaps." It is my mother's turn to be silent.

"Catch a nigger by the toe, if he hollers let him go. Mau Mau catch a nigger." Donald's voice is getting loud again. He is punching the tree trunk with his right hand. My father is walking down the garden holding a glass out in front of him. It is like watching a car crash the moment after the brakes screech and now it is silent, the cars are sliding into each other and there's nothing anyone can do except wait for the sound of the metal crumpling. He takes Donald's shoulder and turns him so I can see his profile. There is another pause then I see my father's hand go back with the glass and the water and the ice hit Donald's face. "Faggot," he yells. Then he shakes his head and wipes his face with his arm. My father is standing there still holding the glass.

Underneath the balcony people are laughing and talking again. I know what faggot means. Christopher told me. Jonas called Christopher a fag and Christopher hit him. That's what his father told him to do. My father didn't hit Donald. Donald's wife is June. She is walking down to the lagoon now. She lurches from side to side as if she is drunk too. The grass is wet. Her heels sink into the ground so with every step she has to pull them out. She is wearing a pale green floaty dress, it looks like a lot of thin curtains. When she gets to them my father speaks to her. I know he is telling her she had better drive Donald home. Then all four of them walk up to the house, my father and Gabriel on either side of Donald, and June limping along behind them. They don't go into the house, they go around the side by the kitchen.

"It's just as well this is the new police commissioner," I say out loud. My voice sounds grown up. Now I know what June's dress reminded me of. The last police commissioner arrived early for a cocktail party. His name was Mr. Eke. He walked through the

French doors. Red went and put his teeth around his ankle. Mr. Eke began to yell but he didn't move. He stood there with the curtains blowing out around him like a skirt and Red crouched, growling softly. Red was looking at my mother. My mother nodded. Red sank his teeth and Mr. Eke screamed. "Red," shouted my mother, "stop it." She went and dragged him off by the collar. "Bad dog," said my mother. He wagged his tail. "Take him up to your room and lock him in there," she said to me. "Oh God, Mr. Eke, I'm so sorry. He didn't know you weren't a burglar. Please come with me. Let me see how bad the wound is. He has had all his rabies injections."

Mr. Eke had tears on his cheeks. He eyed Red and Red growled. "Take him upstairs. Now," said my mother, and I did.

"For God's sake darling, why did you nod?"

"I know. Aren't I awful?" My mother giggled. "I couldn't resist. I wanted to see if Red really had been trained."

"Oh God," said my father, "this could cause terrible ructions."

"I know," said my mother, "I was awful. I just couldn't resist." She put her arm around my father's waist and looked up at him. Sometimes he looks very tall when she stands next to him. He shook his head but he was looking down at her and there was a shine in his eyes and in hers. Even thinking about it I feel weird.

She tells that story of how she nodded a lot and she always says at the end, "Aren't I awful?" and she smiles and when my father's there he shakes his head but he isn't angry.

Dream

We are in the speedboat, my mother and father and brother and me. We are standing up and smiling. We are all wearing bright new toweling shirts. The water is shining. I am standing on the jetty. Something is moving under the water. I want to scream but the sound won't come. I want to warn them. I am in the boat and on the jetty. No one is screaming. Everybody is smiling.

Bats

I am lying awake listening to the air conditioning buzz and chug. I think of fruit bats swinging in wide arcs through the garden. Jeremiah wrapped the bananas already. They're called Egyptian fruit bats. Black shadows crossing the desert, the whole Sahara, they are flying south to King Edward's Road, their sonic beepers twittering. They are hungry for the yellow flesh of bananas. I wait until I can smell the bananas, not quite ripe, before I let myself go on. The great clusters of fruit hang pale in the moon, I can smell the lagoon. Snakes rustle in the bougainvillea and, down between the canna lilies with their veined leaves, the refuse the lagoon brings slaps against the stones. Crabs hurry to investigate, blue pincers ready. At last the bats arrive. They cut dark slivers from the thick air. I want to go and tear the plastic from the fruit for them but I am afraid. They are angry. They have been cheated. They circle above the house, casting spells with their leathery wings, bones like dead fingers showing through the thin skin. They have hollow bones like birds.

It is time. I move the covers to the wall and slide out of bed, checking my brother's face. He is like Red when he dreams, his mouth twitching and his eyes fluttering. I can see him because all night he keeps a lamp on by his bed. Sometimes he sits bolt upright and yells one short yell like a bark of surprise and then he lies back down to sleep. I pick up my flip-flops and very slowly open the door. When I am downstairs I put them on in case I step on a cockroach.

From the fridge I take a scoop of butter. When I close the door I wait until I can see again before making my way to the dining room. They are there, staring straight ahead. I am nervous tonight because there are two new ones, two women, shorter and blacker than the others. They are always angry when they first arrive so I bow my head to them first. I catch myself in a wish. I wish my mother would stop bringing them into the house. I am sorry for this wish. The butter is melting in the palm of my hand and sliding between my fingers. A drop lands on my toe. I stick my left forefinger in the butter and I draw a shape like an eye on the forehead of the first figure. I say, "Do not be angry. Protect us from the dark spirit with red eyes and the ones with holes in their eyes. I welcome you to this house. I bring you offerings." I do the same to each of the figures, always following the same order. I have to be careful to say everything the same way so nobody will be jealous. Then I step back and I bow to each of the six figures in turn. They look out at me from the sideboard. The eye shines on the forehead of one of the women. Moonlight fills the room.

Marine

A typewriter," I say, "a *petite* typewriter." My throat hurts like I swallowed something too big. On the wall over Dave's shoulders are hand marks where we do push offs. "So I can wear stupid shoes and have long fingernails and be a secretary before I get married. Which I'm not going to."

Dave is opening and shutting the case.

"I wanted a rucksack. Or a tent. Mum said they asked before they came to visit. I told her what to tell them."

"Did she?"

I shrug. The typewriter sits on Dave's bed like a spider. A nest of spiders with shining legs and alphabet teeth.

"I saw a dead baby," I say. The words surprise my mouth.

Dave turns the key in the lock. "Where?"

"In the lagoon. It was floating."

"Why?" She turns the key the other way.

"Why what?"

"Why didn't it sink?"

"It was on a mat of palm fronds."

"Why did it die?"

"I don't know."

"Did you touch it?"

"No. The tide took it away."

Dave is frowning. She isn't looking at me, she is looking into the case again which has a ruffly blue lining. "You can lock this," she says, "you can keep things in it."

"Like what?"

"Secret things. Equipment."

I have a belt and a flashlight and a knife. She closes the case and locks it. *Petite Typewriter* it says in blue on the hard cream plastic.

"Wait here." She goes out of the room.

I am thinking about the baby which is being carried out to sea. It is floating between the hulls of ships. It bobs up and down among the bottles and the oil drums.

When Dave comes back in she hands me a big blue magic marker. I cross out *Petite Typewriter* and I write *Jake's Marine Equipment.*

Dave says, "Marines aren't sailors."

"In England they are."

She draws a picture on the case of a sailor with his kit bag. He is walking towards his ship. He is whistling.

Benin

In front of me are a bell and a light. The light makes shadows all around. I step from rock to rock. I'm in a shadow canoe. The bell is a buoy warning the sea. The sea is a sea of snakes. Behind me I hear Red's collar clinking.

"Night adders," says my father. "Puff vipers."

We have reached the veranda. His shadow dances with the night watchman. The house smells green and moldy. The smell sticks to my skin. Now I smell paraffin. Skin in Benin paraffin Benin skin in skin in Benin. The words rock wildly with the shadows. The watchman sets the light down on a table and we're inside a still yellow pool. In the pool are four chairs, a table, and an armchair. The armchair is plump like a mushroom, it is electric blue with purple flecks. Every leg of every piece of furniture is sitting in its own tin can. The paraffin is in the cans. It's to stop the termites.

"Oh God," says my mother. "The government has outdone itself this time."

My father is bent over, lighting the other lamps that are lined up on the sideboard. Soon the light spreads up the walls. They are a greenish cream color. My mother takes one of the lamps and walks through a door. There are two thin beds, one against either wall. The mosquito netting is tied back like curtains. I take my bag with my books and put it on the bed next to the bedside light. Bill fell asleep in the car so he's still standing by the table. His face looks like a mushroom too.

My mother says, "You'd better let him have the bed by the light. You know he has nightmares."

"But I want to read at night."

"Who knows when we'll have power anyway." She walks out of the room so it is dark again. I follow her. She stands in the second doorway.

"They didn't even give us a double bed. Jack. Look."

I look past her elbow. It looks like my room except the beds are wider. "Really, the D. of E. is so bloody Victorian."

"Lots of couples prefer single beds."

"Well, I think that's sad, don't you?"

"We'll push them together."

The bell gets louder again. The watchman comes in with the red and white ice chest. He has already brought in the rest of the luggage. My father takes the chest and puts it on the table. He gets out a bottle of tonic and a bottle of gin, two glasses, a lemon, and a knife. He makes two gin and tonics. At the end he puts his hand in the chest again and brings out four ice cubes. My mother gets out two bags of sandwiches. One bag has bacon and tomato for us, one bag has bacon and ketchup for Bill. The bacon fat soaked into the bread on one side and hardened in the tomato on the other. I taste it, white and smooth between the sour seeds. I look at our faces in the lamplight, the four of us. It's an adventure.

We always eat bacon sandwiches on adventures. Mum feeds Red a piece of her sandwich.

I know where I am. I am in Benin. The bedside light is pale yellow now. I reach and turn it off. In Benin they make leopards. They have an Oba who lives in a mud palace.

He is the king. The cement floor is rough under my feet. I get my shorts out of the suitcase and a T-shirt. I don't want anyone else to wake up. Outside the ground is steaming. It smells different than Lagos, thick and starchy sour, like a green banana. On the other side of the compound walls I hear rusty clattering and the sharp ping of a bell. Bicycles. Inside the compound is an oil palm and some buffalo grass. The oil palm is short and hairy. Its leaves are bristly. At the top there are clusters of orange fruit. They hang together on orange stalks. I think about the palm trees by the sea, how tall and gentle they are. Coconut palms. Benin is far from the sea. I walk around the house until I get to the rocks we walked across like walking across a narrow bridge swinging in the wind. Now I see they are flat slabs like stepping stones across a stream. The night watchman smiles at me from his stool by the gate.

"Master and madam are awake?"

I shake my head, suddenly I am shy. He doesn't have any scars on his face. He doesn't look like Christine. His face is huge, like a mask beaten out of metal with holes for eyes.

"What is your name? My name is Henry."

"Anna. Where do the snakes go in the day?"

He makes a movement with his hand. I see a snake spiraling down into the ground. Then his hand is still. I look at the ground but I can't see any holes.

"Little snakes," he says. He holds up his middle finger. That's how thick they are. He looks at me with his head tipped to one side and he laughs. "But very dangerous deadly," he says and he makes his eyes even bigger.

In the afternoon I plant seeds. They are balsam seeds. On the packet they have pink and orange flowers. They have ten weeks to grow before Mum and Bill and I go back to Lagos for school. I dig the ground with the trowel my mother brought. It is soft. I make holes with a pencil and drop one seed in each and then I put the earth back in the hole. I don't believe they'll grow. I think about all the snakes waiting in the ground for night to come. My father is visiting the Oba. Something's going to happen. I keep feeling it. The feeling is a seed, black with spines. I've had it for a long time. I'm going to bury it in the ground with the Balsam. I'll leave it behind in Benin. I make an extra deep hole with the pencil and I wait until I can see the seed, I can feel it between my fingers, then I drop it in and push the dirt back into the hole and I push the dirt down well and I stand on it.

Killings

My father walks into the room with the radio, turning the antenna this way and that. He's been listening for days, bent over, smoking cigarettes, twisting the tuning knob. "Ssh," he says. I hear the tune for the World Service, thin and cheerful in the paraffin heavy air. "Ssh."

This is the BBC world news for the 31st July 1966 at twenty hours Greenwich Mean Time. The announcer's voice is dry and warm as a wool sweater. He is sitting somewhere watching the wind blow English clouds past the window. *Following the military coup in Nigeria on Wednesday in which Lieutenant Colonel Yakubu Gowon took power, there have been disturbances in the north of the country. Killings and looting are widely reported. Sources in Lagos say the situation is tense.*

"Oh God," says my mother, "I hope we'll be able to get back to Lagos."

"Benin's a long way west and south of the trouble spots."

"What's going to happen? This is the second coup this year."

"I don't know." He's rubbing his forehead back and forth with his long fingers, the knuckles thick and wrinkled. "It's a vicious cycle once it starts, coup and counter-coup, executions and atrocities to go with each one. There's no knowing where it will end. The best we can hope for is that Gowon will be strong enough to stay on top, and fair enough not to give the Easterners too much to resent, but it's a Pandora's box."

"What's a Pandora's box?" I ask.

"The kind of box you wish you'd never opened."

"Why?"

"Because once you've opened it you can't get everything back inside the way it was. It's time for you two to go to bed."

"Go on," says my mother, "brush your teeth first."

I fetch the boiled water from the fridge. I look in the mirror when I'm brushing. It's really happening. It was in the news all over the world. There's a killing ghost that's walking in the land. The killing ghost is white, bone white. She smells of dead animals. Under her fur coat she is naked, behind her dark glasses she is blind. There is no color in her eyes. She is walking across the land in her high heels. Babies are impaled on the spikes of her heels. She has no hair, no eyebrows, no hair down there. She rattles skeletons like keys on a chain and hums, she hums as she walks through the land.

Christine

I stand outside the servants' quarters with my catapult, looking at the lizards. They have orange heads and blue bodies. Jeremiah says there is poison in their heads. I stand on the hot gravel and watch them until the wall is a pattern, blue and grey and orange moving in and out and the lines are a whirlpool sucking me in. I dig my heels in the gravel and make it like my eyes are taking a photograph. Click. Stop. But the lines won't stop, they make one giant lizard with two black eyes and half a tail. The eyes are watching me. The lizard tongue flicks at my ears and face. It touches me over and over. It touches my feet and legs and belly and face until all my skin is licked away and I am wet with bleeding.

"Child, what are you doing, standing in the rain like a fool?"

I hear her voice but I can't make my eyes go away from the lizard. It has a horny orange forehead. Its scales are shining.

"Child," she says, "bring yourself here."

My legs feel squat and angled out from my body like the lizard's. I hear my feet in the gravel. I am going into the servants' quarters where I have never been before. Christine stands in the doorway. She is wearing a dark green and pink cloth.

"What has got into you?"

"The the." I can't make the words unstick. I keep walking towards her and she doesn't go away. She puts her hands on me and skin begins to grow again. I cry. It is Sunday. It's her day off. I smell pepper sauce on her skin. I'm inside yellow light. It's like hugging the sun.

"Come," she says, and I walk down the narrow passage. The walls are black with smoke. In the room at the end of the passage there is a metal pot with an orangey yellow mush in it. She takes the banana leaf which is sitting on the ground beside the pot and she puts some of the mush on it. She takes a ladle from another pot and pours a red oily liquid over it. She hands it to me. "Fufu," she says. She goes in the corner and gets herself another banana leaf.

We sit on the floor. No one else is here. They are visiting with friends or family. I watch how she eats with her finger and thumb and I eat too. At first the fufu tastes like hot cotton wool but then it is like mashed potatoes only sweeter, and curry with groundnuts. "Mmm," I say. I know I stood outside because I wanted her to ask me in. My cheeks get red and fat. I don't want her to know that's what I did. "Thank you," I say when I have eaten all the food on my leaf and licked my fingers carefully. She goes to the corner and pours water from a bottle onto her hand. The water runs onto the floor and down a hole. I do the same.

"Come." She pushes through the green bead curtains hanging in the second doorway down. There aren't any windows, only openings in the cement wall high up near the ceiling so it is dark. I see a narrow bed with a green and white cloth covering, a shelf on which there are more cloths and her two white dresses. By her bed is a gin box with a photograph in a bamboo frame. On the floor is a pair of blue flip-flops.

"Sit," she says. I sit on the bed. On the floor too is half a calabash with oil in it and a wick, and beside that is a box of Swan matches. She lights the wick and her cheeks shine gold in between the shadows. I am trying to see the photograph. She picks it up and holds it in front of me. There is a white man with a stringy neck and a big belly. Beside him stands an Ibo woman with a long curved neck. What I see most are her hands which she holds together in front of her. They are huge, much bigger than the white man's. One of his hands is by his side, the other is raised as if he is saying goodbye or making a blessing. In the corner, across his white trousers, is written, "For Ruth, God's faithful servant, from Arthur Scott-Clarke."

"Who is Ruth?"

"She was my grandmother's aunt."

"Who was Arthur Scott-Clarke?"

"He was the first missionary in the village where she lived, which was Idumuje Ubok. In that village lived also Adagu her sister, the mother of Akueke my grandmother."

"Akueke who never told the secret?" I wait. Christine is sitting on the floor. I can't see her eyes.

"Adagu now was the wife of Chiaku and this had been so for many years. Adagu had brought Chiaku sons and daughters and they worked the land of Chiaku's husband."

"Chiaku's husband?"

"Yes. Chiaku was nwunye di, a woman husband.

"Chiaku was a woman and Adagu was a woman and they were married?"

"Yes. Custom allowed. And in this time it is said Chiaku and Adagu were as friends of an age together. They laughed and hit their thighs from morning to night and there were always yams in the barn. Ruth too then, her name was Uduoga. She was many years younger than Adagu and often she was in their obi for in the house of her father there was little to eat. Many men in the village thought of her. She was strong and beautiful and soon she would be of marrying age. Then the white man came and he made a building. He paid many cowrie shells for it and he hired Uduoga to sweep it clean and make his food. Many in the village said she was not yet ready to be a wife but her father was a poor man and the white man was old and he was rich though he did not have wives or any children. The people then did not understand the Christian way but they worshipped the old gods except Uduoga who was called Ruth. And Ruth then went to her sister's house and she begged her to come into the church with her and be washed clean of her sin.

"'What is my sin?' said Adagu. Ruth stood up straight and she said out loud, 'It is a sin for a woman to marry a woman. There is only one true marriage which is between one man and one woman.' 'It is a sin then for a man to have many wives?' said Chiaku's husband, rolling his eyes toward his first wife. 'Yes,' said Ruth and they all laughed at her then and said one to another, 'She is mad.' But Ruth said, 'No, you must listen to me. As I love you, save yourselves.'

"Chiaku's husband, who was feared by any wrongdoers in the village for his clever questioning, said, 'And now Uduoga, tell me, does the white man say it is good for the husband to divorce his wife?' 'No,' said Ruth and he clapped his hands together for palm wine and everybody laughed again. 'Uduoga,' he said, 'You must ask the white man, what shall we do then, we who are blessed already with many wives?'

"And so Ruth went away and she did not again visit the obi of her sister, instead she stayed in the church. When the people of her village asked her where were her children she told them she was not married to the white man, she was a servant of God. She was called the one who will not marry and her father, though he tried in many ways to find her a husband, he could not and he was sorry he had taken cowrie shells from the priest."

"And what happened to Adagu and Chiaku?"

"They laughed until they died. The old ways are gone now."

"Why do you have a photograph of Ruth?"

"Child, it is time for you to go."

She stands up from the floor and I stand up too. "Thank you for telling me the story."

"Go now," she says and her voice is angry.

In the entrance to the servant's quarters I stop. The light shining off the gravel hurts my eyes. I forgot it was daytime. It has stopped raining. I can feel her eye pushing me out. I left my catapult on her bed. I walk across the gravel. It is a long way. I don't look at the lizards. I go into the house and I hear the sound of T.V. from the study. On Sundays we are allowed to watch *Mission Impossible* but it is almost over when I sit down.

News

The sixth of July, 1967, sixteen hours Greenwich Mean Time. In Nigeria today, the first shots were fired in what the Federal Military Government is calling a "police action" against the breakaway Republic of Biafra.

Help

The water is brown and warm around my shins. Crabs shift under my feet. My sneakers are heavy, they slip off my heels at each step. I hear the crack of a whip. They can't see me. They're in front of the house. They laugh. The water is warm as the air. The air is brown. There are no lights anywhere. My breathing is loud, like water running over rocks.

I hear a scream and then another. The voice slips in between my skin and muscles. Christine. I stop. There's no scream, only the soldiers chanting. They sound like bees, like the bees that chased my father. I am standing listening to the lagoon wash over the rocks at the bottom of our garden. It is so dark I can't see where the water ends and the air begins. It is all warm and brown. She is holding me. I smell her, pepper and green growing vines, wrapped around me, her arms holding me strongly, the lines of her tribe against my cheek. I am listening to her heart. Parrots call in the jungle, a drum tells the news, village to village. Christine. Christine. My nose pressed to her belly I can hardly breathe it's so warm, our skins are mixed together. In her heart drum I can hear voices calling, singing almost, Christine, Christine the Ibo, we want Christine the Ibo. I open my mouth and the dark comes pouring in. Help. I have to get help. I have to be quiet. Hurry. Get help. How long did I stand here? The water is thick against my legs. I must have passed the hedge by now. I should be able to see Peg and Brian's. There should be light from the lanterns. It is dark. I am on a secret mission. I am behind enemy lines. I have to hurry. My skin and muscles are separate now. My muscles move, smooth as snakes. My skin feels the things that float in the lagoon. In the closet in my parents' bedroom Christine is praying. She is praying,

> Our Father which art in heaven
> Debe m ndu Ji rue nne Omumu bea
> Omumu bea

My mother's dresses hang down around her. It smells of perfume in there. My mother and Bill are standing in the upstairs corridor. They are looking down at the soldiers. I climb over the rocks onto Peg's lawn. My shoes squelch and splash. They will hear. I leave them and run, the balls of my feet pushing off the grass. I am in the air, running. I run to the hole in the next hedge. I lie on my belly and crawl. Things rustle. A thorn catches my calf. There is light, quiet and yellow, in Alex's house. The servant is holding a hurricane lamp. It hisses. The light breaks into rainbows. "Help," I say, "help." I am crying now, the tears are on my skin, rolling down it. My muscles are still running and running across the grass.

Trousers

I hear footsteps in the hall. I lie with my arms by my side and my eyelids don't move. I am asleep. Bill went to sleep a long time ago. The door opens. She turns on the light.

"Goodnight," she says. Her voice is thin.

I won't look. She walks to the chair. My father is away. He's away. He isn't here. He went away. He went away to look at war. The war. He's away. She picks up something.

She's in the middle of the room. I want to go away. Everywhere in my body I want to go away. I want to go away anywhere. I want to go. She's standing still. She's looking at me. I won't look. I can feel her eyes sucking on my cheeks.

"If you want to be a man, you have to learn to fold your trousers properly. Look at this, a crumpled mess."

I won't. She knows. I won't. I won't look.

"If you want to be a man you have to learn to fold your trousers properly. IF. YOU. WANT. TO. BE. A. MAN. YOU. HAVE. TO. LEARN. TO. FOLD. YOUR. TROUSERS. PROPERLY."

I open my eyes. Bill will wake up. She is standing by the chair.

She is holding my jeans in front of her. She holds them upside down so the belt buckle dangles down. She pinches together the two legs so the seam is on the side. Her eyes don't have anything in the middle. I feel sick. She shouldn't know. I don't want her to know anything. I live on an island.

"LOOK. AT. ME."

She is still holding them by the bottom. Now she flips them up over her arm. They lie over her arm with the seam facing me.

"There," she says. "There." She smiles at them. "Do you see? DO. YOU. SEE."

"Yes."

"Yes what?"

"Yes thank you."

"Yes what thank you?"

"Yes Mum thank you."

She goes to the closet and gets out a hanger. I can't breathe. She hangs up the jeans and she slides the closet door shut. I close my eyes. I am asleep. I think she can hear my heart.

"Goodnight." She is near the door.

"G'night." I mumble it. She shuts the door. The light is still on. She's gone. I think about her fingers on my jeans. It makes me sick. It. Makes. Me. Sick. Bill hasn't moved at all. I don't know if he is asleep. I wish Dad would come home. I send him a thought in the air. To Biafra. He's flying in a plane with Prince Richard. It is dark except for the green light of the instrument panel. They are sitting close together in the little airplane. Prince Richard is steering. It is too dark to see except when a gun fires and then the ground is covered in dead bodies and the animals are taking legs and arms away in the bush to eat and the animals' eyes are green and shining. Prince Richard and my father fly back and forth. Nobody can shoot them. I get up and turn out the light.

Mask

My father is reading the *Times,* Prince Richard is wearing the crocodile mask. It has a long red and yellow checkered snout and black teeth. He brought it from the war as a present. After he takes it off he says to my mother, "She has your eyes, my dear. She'll be quite a beauty when she grows up. Just like her mother." I feel my mother squirm. She smells like seaweed. He crouches down in front of me, his face sweaty from dancing around the room, and on his cheeks there are red lines where the mask pressed down. His eyes grow big. "Little Anna, if I wait for you will you marry me?" I can't stop looking at the marks on his face. His lips are wet. "Say yes, beautiful Anna, say yes." Everything smells green and slimy. He turns his eyes away for a moment. He looks at my mother. I do too. The middles of her eyes are big and black.

"I'm not going to get married," I say to her and my voice comes out loud but I can't move.

"I'll wait for you," he says, "you'll see, I'm patient."

"No," I say, "I'm not going to get married." Tears are in my throat. My belly hurts.

"Don't be silly," my mother says, "a prince just proposed to you." She is still looking at him. My father turns the page of his newspaper.

House

I am in the hedge building a house the first day Michael comes. Jeremiah went away like Christine did. He was an Ibo too. Michael is a Yoruba. His eyes are bright like the sun on the lagoon and his hands are wide. I can see how his muscles are strung to his bones. He smiles but I don't look at him. All I want to do is build a house. I am going to live on an island alone. Michael weeds the flower beds, his head bobbing among the canna lilies. I build my house out of sticks I weave together and then I lay banana leaves on top.

In the morning the leaves are yellow and covered in swarms of small black flies. They smell dead. Michael is trimming the oleander with his machete. He comes over to me and he says, "You want me to show you how to make a growing house?" I nod my head. He takes some of the longer branches of the oleander and he sticks them in the ground in a circle. He goes to the edge of the lagoon and he brings back an old tin can with no top and no bottom. He looks at me then he holds the can as high as me in the middle of the circle and he ties the tops of the branches around the tin. He has string in his pocket. He cuts it on the machete. "Chimney," he says. On the side facing the lagoon he left a gap. Now he takes two shorter branches. He plants them and ties their tops together.

"A door?" I ask. He nods. He weaves a few of the side branches in and out of the uprights.

"Finish," he says. I look at it. You can look all the way through it. He squats down on the ground and looks in my face. "Three weeks," he says and smiles. His teeth are square and white. He goes back to trimming the oleander.

I sit inside the house. Something hurts inside me. The question starts in my head, "If I can't see you, can you see me?" It is like having a mosquito inside my skull. It is a stupid question but I can't stop having it. I can see myself having it but I can't stop it.

I want it to be quiet inside my head so I sit and I look at one of the branches Michael planted. I feel the bark on the stick and the green juice, how it goes down into the ground and then it is growing a root down and down. I make my mind be at the tip of the root like a little eye until all I can see is blackness. Then I see my twin. I don't see him but I know he is there. I don't feel surprised. I say I'm sorry he died but he won't look at me. He is angry he died instead of me. He doesn't have a body to live in or a house. I say he can live in mine with me. Then it is dark again and my ankle itches. I open my eyes. There is a huge mosquito bite there. It is like a dream but it isn't a dream. It begins to rain but I don't care. I sit in my house with the rain running down my face.

Microscope

Bill has a sick bat. He keeps it in a cage. It has big grey ears. He keeps it in the cage the love birds used to live in. They were called Jack and Jill. Whenever they escaped they flew into the mango tree outside our bedroom window. The tree is full of ticks so we aren't allowed to climb it. Jeremiah climbed it with the cage hooked over one arm. He put seeds in the cage and the birds would sidle along the branch and look at him and then climb right in. I never understood that. Inside the cage all they did was look in the mirror. They had red cheeks and green heads. I couldn't tell them apart. They were in the house when we arrived. My mother said they were sweet. She said when one of them died the other one would pine away and die too and it did.

Bill puts a slice of banana in the cage every day for the bat. The banana goes black and gooey in the bottom of the cage but the bat just hangs upside down and doesn't move. I say, "It eats flies anyway, not bananas," but even when the flies swarm over the banana it doesn't move.

Now the flies have begun to eat the bat. My father says it has to go. He said it before but this time he means it. Tomorrow Michael will bury it.

Bill is in Mum and Dad's bedroom. It is Sunday. He goes there every Sunday morning. I scrape cells from the inside of my mouth with my fingernail. I put them on a slide and add a drop of pinky-orange dye. I fit the rectangle of glass under the clips on my microscope and turn the little mirror so it catches the light. When I look it is like a kaleidoscope but all the same color, each cell with a little dot in the middle. The nucleus. These are dead cells which come out of my body. Bits of my body are dead.

I like looking down the microscope. It's like looking into another planet. I pull out a strand of hair and put it under the lens. I can't see the hair yet, only dust floating. I don't know which way my fingers should go. When the hair does appear in the little circle of light it cuts the circle in half. It is too thick to see through. I have already looked at the shrimps' eggs and the butterfly wing that came with the set.

I go to Mum and Dad's bedroom door. I crouch down and I look through the keyhole. Even before I look I can hear Dad snoring. He is lying on his back. His feet stick up through the sheet. The power is off so they are inside the mosquito netting. The netting makes everything look soft. Mum is lying on her back too. She has her arm around Bill. He is all scrunched up by her side with his head on her shoulder and one arm across her bosom. She is wearing a beige nightdress with lace on the front. His mouth is wrinkled to one side. Nobody moves. I can see where he's dribbled on her shoulder. I am watching from outer space. On planet Earth it is warm. I don't want to look anymore. I have a hole in my belly. It is black. I wait for the black to get bigger and bigger. I can't make it stop. The black is folding in and in. The bed inside the netting gets wobbly like a boat in the harbor when a ship passes. I can hear the wake hitting the side of the boat. It is me crying. I am watching. My knees hurt but I can't get up.

I crawl away from the door and down the corridor. Each tile is enormous, as big as half my body. A black one, a white one, a black one, a white one. When I reach my bedroom the handle is as tall as my father. I can't make any words come. One of my eyes is in the ceiling. It says, "Cry baby, you look silly. Stupid."

The black in my belly splits open. Everything hurts. I am standing on Grandpop's knee. Everyone is looking at my mother. I don't have any clothes on. She is standing against the mantelpiece. Her eyes look like she is asleep but they are open. My grandmother's voice says, "Look at this child. Just look at this child." Something starts to shake inside. I can hear a screaming but it isn't in my mouth. I'm black inside. There isn't anything there. There aren't any edges. The eye in the ceiling says, "Go to sleep. Go to sleep now." It is my twin.

"What on earth are you doing out on the landing?"

My mother's voice. She opens my bedroom door. She takes my hand. It is cold and rubbery. "Did you have a nightmare darling?"

The twin says, "You can get up," so I do but I can't open my eyes.

My mother says, "Poor darling, what's the matter? You can tell me."

Suddenly I can smell her, thick and salty sweet in my nose. I can feel her eyes on my skin. Her face is a spider, black, with jewels. Her legs are moving. She is hungry.

"Come on now, we're going to the beach, don't you remember? Hurry up and get dressed."

I force my eyes open. She is smiling. Her eyes are green and her skin is tanned. The hairs on her lip are blonde. She bleaches them with hydrogen peroxide. She is my mother. She is smiling.

"Bacon for breakfast," she says, "your favorite." She draws the curtains and then she goes down the corridor. I start crying. I can't stop. My eyes are funny. There are bars on everything, light and dark, light and dark.

High

We are in the casuarina tree, smoking its needles through a straw.

"Christopher said banana peels work too, if you dry them well enough." A coconut is bobbing on the oily surface of the lagoon.

Dave sucks hard at the straw then coughs. "Well this isn't working."

"How do you know?"

"Because your eyes go red and you get real hungry and everything looks different and you laugh a lot."

"Different how?"

I know she knows because her sister Jenny did it once and Dave caught her and made Jenny let her try it out. I try to imagine Jenny with red eyes seeing things differently but I can't. She presses her shirt every day for school and she wears her hair in a ponytail high up on the back of her head. I want to know what it's like to see things on drugs.

Dave passes me the straw. "The edges of things look different," she says.

"Now?"

We are looking at Red, who is sitting on the veranda. He yawns and lies down.

"No," she says, "this isn't working."

"I see things different anyway," I say.

"Oh yeah? Like what? What's that?" She points at the coconut.

"A coconut."

"Looks that way to me."

"That's not what I mean."

"What do you mean?"

I can't say anything because I can't breathe and it is dark. Then I say, "Sometimes I go up to the ceiling and I watch everything that happens. Did you ever do that?"

"Like what kind of things?" Dave pinches out the sparks at the ends of the needles.

"I don't know. Just everything." I know that isn't good enough. "Like when you're snorkeling and you look down at the bottom of the sea and you see a stone and the stone moves and it's a fish, a poisonous fish not a stone. You're swimming above and you can see everything is moving, nothing looks like what it is."

"You're weird. Let's go capture Jerry and Bill."

We tie them to the washing pole. "You're the enemy," I say, "and we're going to torture you." I speak to Dave in code.

"We're going to paint you with honey and leave you for the ants unless you tell us the secret," she says.

Bill looks like he is going to cry.

"We're not telling you anything," says Jerry. "You're girls."

"Oh yeah," says Dave. "Take that back." She tickles Jerry in the ribs until he chokes. "Take it back."

He shakes his head so she tickles him again until he says, "O.K., O.K. I take it back."

"So now," I say standing very tall, looking at both of them, "tell us the secret or else." I take a handful of mud from the flowerbed and hold it very close to Bill's face but I don't touch him with it. Waiting is the worst part. Dave practices karate chops around Jerry's head.

"I'm going to tell Mum on you," says Bill.

"Cry baby. Tell-tale. You know what happens to tell-tales? Your eyes will fall out and your tongue will grow so big there won't be room for it in your mouth and it'll hang out." I stick my tongue out all the way down to my chin and let dribble run off it.

Dave says, "Let's go and leave them here."

"Yeah," I say, "I guess they're just lackeys who don't know anything anyway." We begin to walk away. Bill is crying in little baby snorts. Jerry doesn't cry. "Tell you what though, if we set them free they could gather information for our side."

"Even if it just sticks to them."

"Like ants in honey."

"Cos they're too dumb to get it any other way."

"Why not?"

Dave turns to them. "We have decided, just this time, to release you. Next time you'd better have more information."

"Well, what do you say?" I stop in front of the knot. "Well? Say thank you."

"Thank you," Bill mumbles.

"Gee, thanks." Jerry says it sarcastically but we ignore that because Mrs. Lee's car just turned into the driveway.

After they are gone I climb into the casuarina tree again. I am thinking about Bill's face crying. His lips are curled up and his cheek has red lines on it like he went to sleep on wrinkled sheets and he can't breathe, he's gasping for air. I am a long way up looking down at him. I am saying, "Tell it. Don't tell. Tell it. Don't tell. Tell it. Don't tell." It's like a clock ticking. It's not like my voice at all. The needles have gone out again.

Map

Get out get out get out of my blood get out get out my feet follow the words get step out step get step out step and then I'm running in a circle out and out get out is a drum and I'm running in a circle away from the middle I'm running dancing out get out if I could hold the insides pull them pull them out of me this thing dance out get out get out of me I'm dancing I'm dancing a bowl the faster I get the higher my sides I'm a coil of a bowl on the sand in the sand I'm blood in a spiral a trail going out I lie in the sand the sky circles my head and the waves are coming from every direction. Crazy. Weird. Kid. Crazy weird kid. crazyweirdkid. Is my toe still bleeding? I stand up. There is a map in the sand. A blood map. When the tide comes in the sea will lick it away.

Beach

It is night. I watch Dad's elbow come up through the air and then his hand, shining blue-white as it shoots forward and down again into the darkness. His hair sheds feathers of light each time he turns his head to the right and I know how his mouth twists up to make an o for breathing, every other stroke. Then I lose sight of him between the waves. They rise up like the backs of whales. He is swimming down a silver path the moon makes and his feet leave a trail of phosphorescence. Underneath him the night fish eat each other. The waves crash. They are grinding the rocks to sand. Somewhere in the sea, giant jellyfish swim, their crimson stomachs throbbing inside their see-through bodies. Alex has stopped. I can see his head floating up and down on the waves like a beach ball but Dad keeps swimming down the silver path. My heart is beating the same steady rhythm as his arms and his arms and my heart are in time with the sea.

"I wish," says my mother, "he would turn around. He's going too far."

I know she has been thinking those words for a while.

A cloud covers the moon. The sky comes lower. Everything is louder. The breakers look like teeth. I lose sight of him again. The clouds rumble. A jagged finger of light reaches down and touches the sea. It touches right where my father is but when my eyes shake away the stars I see he is closer than I thought. Lightening plays along the waves and dances in the sky. My father is swimming the fastest I have ever seen him swim and Alex too. They swim until a wave comes and takes them in its teeth and throws them out on the sand.

They drink whisky and shiver in the sticky air.

"My God, darling," my mother says, "I thought you were a goner."

"You did!" says my father.

Alex says, "Jesus H. Christ. I'll never do that again."

I make a fire in the sand in front of the beach hut though my mother says it will pour with rain any minute. My father and Alex sit with towels around their waists and shoulders and I watch my father's hair curl as it dries. When it is dry I see there is a streak of silver over his right ear.

"Look at that," says my mother, "you went grey." He puts his fingers to the side of his head as if he can feel where the lightening touched.

My mother says, "Granny's hair went white overnight the night she heard my father had been killed. Promise me you'll never swim at night again. I like my hair the way it is."

My father is shaking so hard he can't talk. Alex stands up. He goes into the hut and puts on navy blue trousers and a white shirt. I keep looking at my father. His face looks like the bones are showing through. I want to remember everything: the way his forehead makes a bump above his eyebrows, the crow's feet in the corner of his eyes, the way by his nose his eyelids are crinkled as if there isn't enough room for them, his big long nose which curves out in the middle, and the mole on his upper lip which has two hairs growing out of it. In the firelight his eyes are pale grey. All the blue has gone out of them. His teeth are big and square and yellow but his lips don't have an edge really, they fade into his skin. When I look at his lips he looks young. They are like small furry animals and the rest of his face is a cliff, is something the wind carved out of rock. I want to reach out my hand and stroke his lips. He smells of whisky now and salt and something sour. The smell of whisky makes me scared. "Can I have some?"

"No, you're too young," my father says.

When I go to sleep I hear the rain rushing through the palm fronds. In the morning I find a jellyfish with blue tentacles, an orange shell with pale gold freckles, and the armless body of a doll with seaweed tangled in her blonde hair, washed far up on the beach. The sea is green and apricot and purring. We go for a walk after lunch. We walk past Modke and Tanya's hut. They play bridge with my parents sometimes by the light of the hurricane lanterns. Modke is lying on his belly on the sand. Bill says, "He looks like a doormat."

My mother says, "Sssh. Jewish men are very hairy." Tanya is lying on a white beach chair. She is wearing a pale green bikini and she has slices of cucumber on her eyes. Her belly shines like polished wood, it is smooth like driftwood and flat like someone poured oil into the bowl her hipbones make. In the early mornings I see her and Modke running up the beach, side by side. They met when they were in the army in Israel. Sometimes they look after other people's children. This weekend they have Sam and Katie's son Josh staying with them. I know who Sam is. He is the director of Kingsway. He is a Yoruba. He comes to cocktail parties and he wears a suit. He went to Cambridge. Tanya and Modke have tied a rope to a life ring and put Josh inside it. He sits where only the longest waves can touch him. The life ring looks like a red and white skirt sticking out from his fat belly. He takes a fistful of sand and watches it dribble out, wet and brown, between his fingers onto his toes. Everyone but me and him and the boy who sells banana ice creams is asleep. I am eating my ice cream from the top and the bottom. Drips keep running down onto my fingers anyway. The part of the stick I can see says, *What is yellow and black and dangerous?* When I try to shake the flies away I lose a bit of the ice cream but I still can't see the answer. I watch the ants try to take away the lost ice cream. Just when they have a grip it melts all over them and they have to stop and clean themselves. I am looking at their eyes when I hear the scream. It is Tanya. Little shapes of people, dark against the white sand, are running towards her. The sand burns the soles of my feet. My father is in the water already. My mother is fastening her bikini top. More people are in the water. They are swimming everywhere. The life ring lies on the dry sand. It is empty. Tanya wants to swim too but people won't let her so she stands on the beach and stares at the sea.

"Oh my God," says my mother. "She'll never forgive herself."

I am still holding the ice cream stick. It says, *Shark's fin custard.* The men are still swimming. The women walk up and down the beach looking for the body. My mother stays with Tanya.

The young man with one foot limps across the sand to us. It takes a long time. All the other men are out in the canoes fishing. He looks at Tanya with his red eyes. "Yemaya has taken him," he says. "She is a cruel mother. Tonight when the moon shines you will see she spread her hair across the waters."

Tanya doesn't seem to hear. She keeps staring at the sea and squeezing her hands together. "They'll find him," she says. "They must."

The man says to my mother, "It is not good to swim now. She is angry."

My mother says, "The body must be found." He makes a movement with his hand and arm, which I know means the undertow is here. He shakes his head and hobbles back toward the shade of the palm trees. I count the number of heads bobbing in the sea. When the sun goes down, the men swim back in and the women walk back along the beach. Modke is grey and shaking.

"How can we tell them?" he says. "Their only son."

"It was an accident," my mother says.

"What difference does that make?" says Modke.

Tanya doesn't say anything. She sits and holds her legs and looks at the sea. The red in her eyes makes her irises look pale green like her swimming costume.

They go back to Lagos in their boat and the moon shines on the sea. It is like hair spread silver across the waves and like the silver path my father swam down.

Wake

"I went to the wake today."

"Oh yes?" says my father, wiping cream from his chin.

"It was hot and dark and smelly. The women sat there and wailed. Katie sat wrapped in blue traditional dress and wailed with the best of them. She looked exhausted. It goes on for days and days. I'd never have guessed she would go back to the old ways. She looked like any other Yoruba village mammy. Carol said the same thing. She said it's especially hard for them not having found the body because the Yoruba believe the spirit can't rest till the body is properly buried. But really it was so odd to come out of that room into the light and see Sam sitting there in his dark suit reading the newspaper. In a way though I think Katie will get over it quicker. Carol said when John's mother died he went back to the village. Left her in the city with three young children. But when he came back he was over it. I don't think it's been easy for Carol. A little red headed lass from Birmingham married to a strapping black man. She says her mother almost died."

"Why?" I ask.

My mother rings the bell for Gabriel to clear the plates.

"Why did she?"

"Well, can you imagine?" My mother is waiting for Gabriel to go back in the kitchen. "I don't suppose I would be thrilled if you married a Nigerian."

"Why not?"

"It's not the color of their skin, that's not it, it's the cultural difference. I just don't think it works very often. You don't expect the same things. Anymore than if you married a Yorkshire miner."

"I'm not going to get married anyway."

"Don't be daft. You'll grow up and marry a rich man and keep your mother in her old age, won't you darling?"

Gabriel brings in the coffee and the cream and the sugar.

"I won't get married."

"You wait and see. You'll fall in love with someone just like Dad fell in love with me."

My father takes the *Times* out of his briefcase. The paper is thin and crispy. It is the kind they send by airplane. On the page facing me, in small black letters, it says: *Starvation in Biafra.* Christine is in Biafra. He puts the paper down and lights a cigarette. When he picks it up again he folds it in half. I can't see the article. I can't see him, only his hands and the smoke coming out of the top of the paper.

I know my mother is going to tell the story again but I always listen. There is something I keep missing.

"Before I ever met Dad I was one of the entertainment secretaries at the Foreign Office. It was our job to organize parties as well as doing ordinary secretarial work. They gave us a hundred pounds extra a year for clothes and expenses. That was a lot of money in those days. Brigitte did it too. We shared a little cottage right by Hyde Park where the Horse Guards exercised their horses in the morning. It happened that I had to give a party for Princess

Christina of Sweden. I was at my wits' end. She was six feet tall and all my boyfriends were in the Horse Guards, little chaps. Then Brigitte said, 'What about that tall young man who tips his bowler to you in the tube?'"

"That's Dad," says Bill.

"'He works in the Foreign Office, doesn't he? Ask him.' So I invited him and the party was a great success. The only thing was they danced for hours and I ran out of Pimms but I thought, God, they're all so drunk they'll never notice if I give them cold tea instead. So there I was in the kitchen brewing up gallons of black tea when who should walk in but Dad. That's when he decided this is the wife for me, isn't it darling?"

"Yes," says my father. He gets up. He puts his hand on her shoulder and squeezes it. Then he goes over to the radio. The bells of Big Ben sound. Seventeen hours Greenwich Mean Time. "So what happened after that, after he decided that?" I ask.

"Hush," says my father. "The news."

Baby

At the bottom of the ocean there's a baby. It begins like this. The baby is dead in the ocean. In the ocean the baby is dead. The baby has no bones. It is little and wrinkled and it smells. The bones are away by themselves. They dance. When there is drumming baby bones dance through the dark and in between the guns the bones which don't have any eyes are looking. They are looking at every single person and if that person is face down dead they, the bones, burrow down into the earth and they come up looking in that dead face. The bones have been doing this for a long time. They are old bones. They're looking into people's eyes to find the place where people go when they go away when they go away in a secret place when they go away the bones are looking for that place.

Dark

I listen to the tablet drift down through the water and then clunk, hit the bottom. I listen to the fizz. It's a white sound. The bottle of Alka Seltzer sits on the sideboard with the malaria pills, under the Ibejis. After she has drunk the Alka Seltzer Mum takes two codeine. Dad eats a piece of toast. The piece of glass I covered in soot yesterday is leaning up against my chair. I moved it back and forth over the candle just above the pointing tip of the flame until the whole glass was black and when I looked at a light bulb it was dim and brown like looking through dirty water. I am afraid we will be late but I don't say anything.

At school everyone is standing in the playground. There are eight hundred and twenty of us. Mr. Rice says, "An eclipse happens when the moon passes in between the earth and the sun, hiding the sun from view. In the past, and for many primitive peoples around the world today, an eclipse is viewed as a fearful supernatural omen. An eclipse, however, is produced by strictly natural causes and may be predicted with certainty by astronomers."

Mrs. Welt says, "Remember, only look at the eclipse through your shadow boxes or through smoked glass. Looking directly at an eclipse can burn your eyes."

I am standing next to Christopher. He keeps fidgeting. "What's the matter?" I whisper. His skin looks tight on his face. He is wearing long pants. "Did you get beat last night?" He looks away. Then he nods his head. There are tears in his eyes. Something goes red and hot inside my chest. I kick a stone and hit Matthew on the back of his leg. He turns around. His eyes are wide and brown.

"Hey," he says, "hey." I know he won't do anything.

"It's beginning," says Mr. Rice.

I look up and I see a little shadow cutting into the sun then I can't see anything. I have to look at my feet. Everyone is holding something in front of their eyes, looking up. I look through the smoked glass. Something is eating the sun. The sky is darker and darker. Is this how it would be to go blind? Now the sun shines only on the edges. The middle is black. I can hear my father singing "Brown Skin Girl." Mr. Rice is talking someplace. I'm waiting for the hole in the middle to grow until there's no light at all. Christopher is waiting too. When it is black everyone will fall down on the ground as if we are sleeping. No one will move. We will be dead. After that if the sun comes back everything will be different. My father is still singing, he is still singing *Brown Skin Girl, stay home and mind baby, I'm going away on a sailing ship, Won't be back for many a day*. I look through my glass. I have a hole in my middle. My father's voice is going around and around the edge like someone running their finger round and round the rim of a glass to make it whistle. If you make it whistle high enough the glass will break.

"It's over," says Christopher. "You gonna stop looking?"

"Hey," says Matthew, "That was neat wasn't it?"

Mostly Matthew is O.K. but today I can't stand how his socks are pulled all the way up. I shrug. He has little brown freckles on his cheek like a thrush's egg. He looks like an egg anyway. Quiet like that. I picture somebody picking him up and tapping him on the side of a bowl and all of him running out, slimy and yellow. "What happened?" I say. "Nothing." I like answering my own questions.

He takes off his glasses and wipes them on his T-shirt.

When he puts them back on he says, "You always want things to be different than they are. You'll never be happy."

"So? So what?" I say. He isn't like other kids either. Sometimes he leans back in his chair and puts his hands together on his belly and he says, "I'm exhausted," like he's one hundred and five years old. His grandmother lives with him. I think his mother is dead.

Blow Job

It's a blow job." Dave smoothes the paper on her knee. It is not as thick and shiny as the other ones.

"Is she Korean?" He is big and white. She looks so small.

"No. She's Japanese."

I want to say, how do you know? I want to say, no, she's Korean. I want to fight. "I don't like this one," I say. "I don't want to keep it." I can't stand how her eyes are closed and how his hair is curly down there and pushes against her face. She is wearing lipstick. It looks like someone has drawn it on with a crayon.

The bunker is concrete and it smells of piss. "That's where Dad was chased by the bees," I say, pointing to the fairway. "African killer bees." Between the road and the golf course is a strip of jungle. On the edge of that strip is the bunker. Lizards stick their heads in and blink at us. We call it a bunker but nobody knows what it is for. We are sitting just inside.

Dave turns the piece of paper over. On this side there are mostly advertisements but at the bottom of the page there are words. She reads aloud. "He picked her up and held her over his huge throbbing cock. 'Oh baby yes,' she whimpered. 'Fuck me, fuck me.' 'Slut,' he grunted and thrust her down on his member. She screamed. 'Take it, cunt, take it.' He thrust harder into her willing—"

"Willing what?"

"Pussy? Twat? Beaver? Hole? I don't know. I don't have the next page." Dave's voice sounds weird, as if it is coming from further inside in the dark. "Then she knelt down and took his pulsing member, no, his organ, between her swollen lips. Your turn."

"It was so big she couldn't breathe." I can't go on. "I don't want to keep it," I say. "Let's burn it." Dave looks at me, I can feel her eyes, but she doesn't say anything. The page is damp where she carried it in the pocket of her jeans. I set fire to it with the matches I always keep in my kit. I watch the paper go black and crumble into pieces. The lipstick doesn't burn. I use another match and it is all gone. The smoke smells thick and sweet.

"Why didn't you want to keep that one?"

"It was dumb," I say.

Dave doesn't say anything. It begins to rain. The rain sounds like bullets on the roof of the bunker. "Come on," I say, and we walk back down the road. My hair gets flat and dark like hers. I like how my T-shirt feels cool and heavy and how the water follows the line of her jaw and drips down her chin. The road is bright orange and all the plants are shining green. We walk with long strides side by side. Jake and Dave, Jake and Dave, Jake and Dave, is all I think.

Soap

I am trying to hold my teeth away from the soap. It is smeared on my tongue. The floor is white and echoing. Mrs. Welt takes the soap from out my mouth. I make her disappear. I look at the long white line of basins. They lead as far as I can see into the faraway and in that place I'm looking back at me. I don't know why I said what I said. The words jumped out of my mouth. I didn't know they were there.

Mrs. Welt says, "Now wash your mouth out. Do you want me to tell your parents? Wash it out."

They're not in my mouth anymore. They're in my head. I bend over the sink and put my mouth in the cold water. The words are printed in my head in thick black pencil. They won't go away. The taste of soap is in my nose. The door opens. I freeze. There isn't time to stand up. My dress is too short. It's a girl in sneakers. Whoever it is doesn't say anything and Mrs. Welt doesn't either. A stall door closes. She is watching me to see how clean I get. The soap won't go away. It's stuck down the back of my throat. I feel my throat close like I'm going to throw up.

"That's enough now," she says but I keep on filling my mouth with water and spitting it out and filling it again. I want it to wash out. Whoever is in the stall still hasn't come out. Mrs. Welt turns off the water. I walk behind her. Her shadow is bigger than me.

In the classroom nobody says anything. My neck is stiff and tall. When I reach my desk I take a sharp left and sit down.

"Now," says Mrs. Welt, "read me what you wrote. Matthew."

Matthew says, "Parents teach their children values."

I look down at my desk. The corner of my paper is folded over. I open it. It says, "Fuck her." I look at Christopher quickly but he's looking at Mrs. Welt, his eyes wide and innocent.

"Honor and obey," says Matthew. He is born again. So are his father and his grandmother. They were all born again the same day. He told me that the first time I beat him in a math test. He shook my hand. That was in the third grade.

I remember that. I don't remember the words coming into my mouth. I don't remember even thinking them. I remember Mrs. Welt wrote on the board, "Social Responsibility." She said, "Adults in our society have many responsibilities. For example, they have the responsibility to vote." Somehow she got onto families. That's where we learn responsibility, like looking after your younger brother or sister. Parents are responsible for their children. "What kinds of things do parents do for their children?"

Joshua said, "They feed them." He never says anything so I remember he said that.

"They buy them clothes."

"They love them."

"They send them to school."

"They give them birthday presents."

"They teach them what's good and what's evil." That was Matthew. After that there was a silence.

"Come on," said Mrs. Welt, "Think of all the things your parents do for you."

"Mothers teach girls how to cook." Caroline.

"Fathers teach boys how to be men." Christopher. That's when it happened.

"Come on now," she said, "they . . ."

"Fuck them."

The words were loud. Nobody even laughed. It wasn't my voice. I wanted to take them back inside, to suck them out of the air, but I couldn't. I watched Mrs. Welt's cheeks go orange and then her forehead did too. Her dress was blue. When her mouth opened she looked like one of the lizards. Her tongue came through the air at me like a lasso. I could feel her spit touching me. "The relationship between parents and children is sacred. I'm going to wash your mouth out with soap." Her hand was half an inch away from my shoulder. It said, "You're too dirty to touch." At the door she said, "The rest of you will write about the responsibilities of parents toward their children and the duties of children toward their parents."

After class Matthew is coming toward me. His eyes are very big like they get when he tells you something Jesus said so I go to the bathroom and I wash my mouth out some more and then I go in the stall and lock it and I eat my sandwich.

House

I go to my house. I crawl inside, pulling the towel back down over the doorway it is dark and hot like being inside the ground the air touches me everywhere it touches in between my thighs it touches my shoulders and my eyes it's like another skin the earth's like a huge body breathing I can feel it breathing I can feel the oleander growing my house thicker and stronger already there's no light that can come in I breathe in the dark and my skin melts away my blood and the dark are a tide flowing in and out like breathing like everything touching all the shores of the earth something glides over my thigh warm and dry it goes on and on like the breathing. It's a snake. It's a snake. It's a snake. I'm not afraid. I keep breathing. It lives here too. It's gone out through the door, sliding through the grass in the daylight. Everyone can see it sliding under the bougainvillea hedge. At night it will come back. This house is its home. I wasn't afraid.

Drowning

Dave shows me how to strangle someone. She puts her fingers around my neck, the thumbs pressing into the soft triangle where my collarbones meet. Then I do it to her. "No," she says, "Stand closer so you can really push down with your thumbs."

The front door opens and closes. It is her father going back to the office. Her mother is shopping. I say, "I almost drowned the other day. It was at Lighthouse Beach and I swam real far out. The black flag was flying but I didn't care. I was swimming along when I felt myself being pulled under. It was like a giant octopus wrapped around my legs and pulled me down. I couldn't breathe. The sea was pushing at my lips saying, let me in, let me in, and my blood was saying it too but I wouldn't open my mouth and the sea was angry. Everything was black. I held my breath but I knew I couldn't hold out much longer. The sea was like a finger pushing at my mouth, opening my lips, and I knew if I let it in I would die. I knew what that meant. It meant I wouldn't be me anymore so I said inside over and over, I'm Jake, I'm Jake. And then I began to remember. My whole life flashed in front of me."

I know Dave is listening. She isn't even chewing the skin on the side of her fingers. I don't know what I will say next. My heart is banging in my throat. "I saw myself when I was five, playing pirates with Bill on my parents' bed. The bed looked big as a field."

Dave wriggles her toes in her high-top sneakers.

I say, "I saw my grandmother's face when she found Sylvie and me playing together."

"Big deal."

"Sylvie was naked and so was I. We were looking at each other down there when I heard footsteps and there wasn't time to get dressed so I pushed Sylvie in the closet and leaned on the door but when my grandmother came in she knew Sylvie was there. She told me to get out of the way and she opened the closet door. Sylvie was inside in the corner with her hands over her eye. She looked so small and white. That was the only time I ever saw Granny get angry."

"Did she beat you?"

"No. And then I remembered being born."

"Aw, come on, you did not."

"I did too. If you remember everything when you're drowning then you have to remember that too."

"Yeah? So what was it like?"

"Dark and red and hot. There was a lot of noise like being inside an engine. I couldn't breathe. It felt like something was wrapped around my throat, pulling tighter. I was trying, trying to get out. I was touched all over and squeezed." I know I shouldn't be telling her this but I have to. The words are pushing themselves out of my mouth. I want to cry but I am a sailor remembering. "I remember the smell, it was thick and sticky, like fufu. Peppery and sweet. And then I was out and everything was shining but I still couldn't breathe and couldn't breathe so they hung me upside down and hit me. "

"So then you sucked on your mother's tits, right?"

The sickness hit me in my stomach like she punched me. "No. I didn't want to." I can feel thick white liquid dribbling out of my mouth. I put my fingers to my face. It's not there. "No. I didn't."

Dave is looking out the window. The rain has stopped. She's moving her left shoulder up to her ear and then back down and around. "So where did you come from?"

"What do you mean?"

"I mean is it the asshole or what?"

"No, dummy, there's another hole. It's called the vagina."

"But that's pussy. Vagina's pussy."

"Shut up."

"You shut up. It's twat. Pussy. Vagina. It's the same thing. It's not big enough."

"Well that's where they come out."

"Let's go outside."

"I didn't finish telling you about drowning."

"O.K., O.K. You didn't drown did you?"

"After I was born I saw mermaids. They were singing to me and waving their hair. I wanted to go with them to where it was dark and slow. The bodies of sailors were lying on the ocean floor with yellow fish swimming in and out of their mouths. I wanted to just float and look at them. But I heard a voice calling my name so I swam back up through the dark to the blue except it was more like pulling myself up on an invisible rope than swimming. When I reached the air I began to cry. The air burned in my lungs. I know when I want to, I can go back down there."

Dave is just looking at me. I think she's going to say you made that up but she says, "You want me to draw you a picture of the mermaids and the sailors?"

I feel warm inside for the first time in a long time.

Christine

"Christine."

She looks at me, rings like bruises round her eyes. "What?"

"The war is nearly over."

She looks at her hands. They seem even bigger now they are just bones and skin. She looks at her fingers as if she is counting them. She says, "Government words can't bring back what is gone."

"Perhaps they're not really gone, perhaps they are hiding in the bush like Akueke did." I say it fast.

"When a hope so slim you can't see him sideways, no good in looking anymore."

"How many children do you have?"

She looks at her hand. "Five. I had five children."

I think about the children in the newspaper pictures with their thin bones and bellies swollen out like they are pregnant. They look at me. Their skin is cracked open. Every night Daniel takes the newspaper to the servants' quarters. Christine's hand looks dead, like something drowned and washed up on the beach. "Do you believe in God?" I say. "Do you pray?"

She looks at me again, her eyes hard.

"Granny says we go to heaven if we're good." When I say it heaven sounds like the Isle of Man, purple mountains and heather and sea mists.

"Heaven," she says. "Our Father which art in heaven." She shrugs. "My people," her eyes are still hard, "believe when someone dies their spirit returns in a new body. Sometimes we can recognize them, we say this baby has the spirit of her great-grandmother."

"How can you tell?"

"Sometimes they favor the same foods, maybe the child knows the old woman' s special song."

"What about twins, what are they?"

"Twins are very bad. When the midwife sees a second baby coming she runs away. She runs about the village sobbing. The village council meets and takes away the twins. The mother goes alone to a place where the mothers of twins are purified. She spends ten market days alone in that hut."

"Where do they take the twins?"

"Used to be they drown them or they throw them into the jungle where the animals will devour them."

My stomach hurts. "Why did they do that?"

"The twin is a sign the parents have committed some crime."

"That's bad," I say. "It's ignorant and stupid."

She shrugs. "The missionaries when they came, they took the twins, they put them in orphanages where they trained them to be servants."

"The Yoruba think twins are special. They make statues of them if they die and give them food."

She shrugs. I stare at the floor. I want her to touch me. I want her to hold me. I can't look at her. I want her to put her arm around me and pull me close to her. She is a miracle. My father said, "It's a miracle she got through." My mother said, "It's a miracle she survived." Christine is a miracle. I want her to tell me a story like she used to, about Akueke or Chiaku. They lived in the secret place she used to go with her eyes. I want to ask her about that place. I want her to go there again. I want her to be fat and strong and holding me. My skin aches from the wanting. I can't look at her face. I look at her hands on her thighs, they are resting on the white dress like birds about to fly off.

"Christine, I have a twin. He isn't dead. He was supposed to be dead but he isn't. He watches everything." My heart is beating hard. "He lives under the water. I go there. It's dark and quiet and I can see. I watch everything above like I'm my twin, like I'm in the place people go when they die and nobody can hurt me or see me or touch me but I can see everything. I wait there for my twin to come to me. I watch him. I never know what he's going to say. He doesn't know either."

She's going to say I'm crazy. Crazy weird kid. It doesn't matter. We're going away. I won't ever see her again. She puts her hand on my back. My chest fills with black water and I'm crying and coughing as if I've been drowning but her hand is warm. It sucks away the black water. She doesn't say anything.

Mirrors

We aren't sailors. We aren't even boys. I am afraid to say anything because I can't remember anything I said before. I make words like spit, so easy. I'm drownng in my own spit. I don't remember how to swim. I don't know where I am. It's like a wave is coming up behind me, right behind me, washing everything away.

I have to go, my mother and my father and my brother and me, we have to leave Nigeria. I don't want to but it's best because you'll find out my lies and then you won't be my friend because I can't remember what stories I've told. If I can't keep the threads in my head you will find one and pull like pulling a loose thread in the hem of a T-shirt and it will all unravel and then you won't be my friend because I have lied, because I don't remember, I don't remember what's true.

Did I see a green mamba in the bamboo did it look at me and look at me did I break a bone did I nearly drown did a snake come to live in my house did Christine ever take me in her room and tell me stories feed me fufu with her fingers did I save her when the soldiers came did I wade through the lagoon in the dark for help did I see a dead baby?

I don't remember the stories I told. I remember the words coming out of my mouth, how they wove together like a web, how they went round and round and stuck to each other, how big and shiny the stories grew.

I am standing in the bamboos. Everywhere I look there are huge spider webs. They run between every single stick and they shine like mirrors. I am fat and thin and tall and short, my face bubbles out and it's like a cave. When I move my hands all my hands move in a crowd, when I open my mouth my mouths say Anna, Anna, Anna.

I am living in a house of mirrors in the dark.
I am living in a house of mirrors in the dark.
I am living in a house of mirrors in the dark.

Sailor

Hey sailor. Boys don't cry," I say. I am Jake and she is Dave. She doesn't ever have to know. I do what Jake would do. I grab her arms and we wrestle. We roll over and over but I let her pin me.

She is still crying, sitting on top of me. "I don't want you to go."

Something aches in my belly. Maybe she knows and she doesn't care that I lied. Maybe she doesn't care. Maybe she doesn't care. The words twist like a snake, green with black eyes. Did I tell her that? I start to cry. I can't stop it.

She puts her hand on my hair and she strokes it. Something thick and black begins to tear me open in all the secret places. It is too big. I want to be empty. I want to be Jake. I push her hand away. "Remember," I say, "when we're grown and free we'll sail around the world together." I make my voice sound like I believe it.

She gets off of me. "Yeah," she says. "Yeah." She goes to her desk and she makes me a cartoon. I look over her shoulder. There is a ship. We carry our kit bags on board. I'm wearing a cap and I stand at the wheel. Dolphins swim around the ship. Stars shine. On an island nearby there are palm trees and a hut with walls made of leaves. She is playing a guitar. The notes hang over the water almost touching it.

Cycle III

***

The Mosquito King

1965–1968

Mother

When I come back she is asleep. She lies on her back with no bikini top, one hand on each breast, sleeping. I stand on her left where my shadow will not cross her. I can see her nipples. They have little bumps and in the middle the little bumps make a cluster. Instead of sticking out the nipple sinks into her breast like a puddle in damp sand. There is a freckle on the left one. Her belly spreads out on either side of the towel. Black curly hairs make a line from her bikini bottoms up to her belly button, a column of ants marching up her, I want to sweep them away. A Jacob's ladder she calls it. A Jacob's ladder is a ladder they hang over the side of a ship so sailors in rowboats can climb on board. Her mouth is open a little like it always is when she sleeps. Through the waves I can hear her snore. Quietly, as if she is dreaming of the quince tree heavy with gold fruit, or picking mushrooms early in the morning, or riding around Ireland on her chestnut mare, which she did when she was seventeen. She slept in barns and ate duck's eggs for breakfast. I look at her nipples again. They are like greedy brown hands. I shake my head. The idea won't go away. They don't belong to her. They are holding on. Parasites. In the sun she smells of mushrooms. I look at the sea, the light and the water moving together, like breathing. It never stops. Sometimes it makes me crazy, breathing all the time, in out, in out. Except when you die. The sea doesn't die. She looks a long way below me, on the towel on the sand. People say I look like her. Her eyes, her nose, her forehead. Straight nose and big eyes. Bug eye, they say at school. A wide forehead, a widow's peak pointing down. Her hair is black, mine is brown like my father's. Her hair is thick and wiry. Italian, she says. The Italian in me. A drop of sweat runs down the middle of her forehead. It reaches the bridge of her nose, dodging her eyebrows. I move my hand over her face, just with one finger pointing out to wipe it away. She opens her eyes. I take my hand away. "A mosquito," I say, "was about to bite you."

"Oh." She smiles and looks at me. Her eyes are green and grey and flecked with gold. "Thank you." She sits up and looks along the beach. She looks puzzled. "What time is it?"

"About four."

"Where are Dad and Bill?"

"Flying the kite. Look."

High up in the blue the yellow tail of the kite flicks and curls, the red diamond making lazy circles. She smiles some more.

"Sit down."

I sit on the sand. It burns my thigh. I wriggle my toes down to where it is cool.

"You're going to be a beautiful young woman."

I look at my legs. The hairs are shining gold in the sun. "You are. You have beautiful eyes."

"Everyone says they're like yours."

I can feel her smiling. "When you were in Ireland did you eat duck's eggs?"

“Oh yes. And milk fresh from the cow still warm, with the cream floating on top. I slept in barns in the hay. Even when the farmer offered me a bed I slept in the hay. I can smell it now. It was so sweet, and Boadicea my horse munched away at it all night.”

“I want to do that one day.”

“Perhaps you will.”

She reaches for the Ambre Soleil and hands it to me. She is lying on her belly now on the towel. I squeeze the cream onto my hands and let it sit there for a moment. I rub it into her shoulders, first one then the other, my hands making circles on her skin, the flesh moving like ripples of water on either side of my hands as I rub the cream down her spine and off to each side.

“Mmmm,” she says.

I kneel and rub all the way down to her bikini bottoms, to the bulge on either side and the snoring starts again. I carry on rubbing until I have used almost the whole tube. I sit back down, wiping my hands on my thighs so they shine too and the sand sticks to them. The kite is overhead now, swinging in huge figures of eight, up and down and up and down and up again, always to the same place, starting over and over, up and down and round again, the red kite in the blue sky with a yellow tail.

Eye

"Christine. There is a bird with one red eye. When the drums play the bird flies in the air between the casuarina tree and the mango tree."

"Silly child, it is a bat after the bananas."

"Does a bat have one red eye and can he see through walls?"

"Come, where did you see this bird, in a story book?"

"I saw him in the mirror."

"True word?" says Christine and she crosses herself.

"It's true isn't it?"

"I do not know. Akueke my grandmother says what is done in darkness is seen. The spirits will tell what is shameful in the obi. The fathers came and washed away the spirits.

"As I am baptized Christine, I do not have the eye of seeing."

Beggar

Black bottoms," says my mother, washing her hands, "that's what you like. You're a dreadful racialist." Red wags his tail. His lip is hooked up over one tooth. His gum is black and pink. He is grinning. She puts away the Dettol and the gauze.

We put towels on the car seats. Where I touch the plastic it scorches my thigh. On the way up King Edward Road I see two children squatting by the side of the road. They are crying. One of them looks up and sees us. His face is dusty and streaked. They run away into the cemetery. I say, "Why don't we just give them some mangoes, then they won't steal them?"

"They'll only want more," says my mother.

We pass the *Guinness Gives You Power* ad and cross the bridge. It's just my mother and me. Bill stayed at home. My father is away. "Where are we going?"

"The Economat and then the market."

The Economat is the French Embassy's shop but we're allowed to use it too. I get out of the car. A man is sitting on the step in front of me. He doesn't have any hands. A tin cup is tied to his arm with a piece of leather. He shakes it so it rattles. Where there aren't any hands the skin makes a crease. The skin is pink like bubble gum and brown, and on his face too he doesn't have a nose, just more pink and brown skin. His eyes look cloudy like a fish's eyes after it is cooked.

"Come on," says my mother.

In the shop it smells of ice and cheese and wine. "Monsieur, le brie, c'est bien?"

"Oui, Madame."

"What made him look like that?"

"Really," says my mother, "please stop talking about it. I'm trying to buy dinner." She is looking at the meat. Some of it is pink and some is brown. When I touch it, it is hard and cold.

"Are there beggars in England? There aren't, are there?"

"No."

"Only in Africa?"

"No, there were plenty in Hong Kong but you don't remember."

When she gets her change back she doesn't put it all in her purse. "Can I?" I say and she gives it to me.

When I step out of the air conditioning it's like walking into soup, like the first time getting out of the airplane, the air brown and sticky pushing up my nose and into my throat, and his cup rattling is like shivering inside. I throw the money in. He keeps shaking it back and forth, his arm with no hand. I look down. He has no feet. The rattling and laughing and honking and bicycle bells fill my ears. I stand, a boat at anchor, the tide coming in, filling the harbor, filling and filling it. I float higher, straining at my chain. Hot rubber and sweat, frangipani, piss, fish, the smells lap around the hurrying shoes of businessmen. Somewhere someone is playing High Life. The music and the smells are weaving into each other, bright as the cloths the women wear on their heads waiting in the mammy wagons, laughing and calling, their heads wrapped in tie-dyed pink and emerald, blue and white, blue and orange. They sit in the open backs of the lorries which are caked in dust, but the women are brighter than the brightest birds. They are big and they are laughing. The cup rattles and rattles.

"Come on," says my mother. "Don't just stand there. The diesel fumes are choking me."

Crabs climb over each other in baskets. Sharks hang from hooks by their gills. Barracudas lie in ranks smiling with their needle thin teeth. I look at the woman standing over them, one hand on her hips. She jingles the money in her apron. She is rich. All the stalls are run by women. She has strong arms. She jokes with a customer as she turns, picks up a basket full of fish, empties it onto the counter. She arranges them, her hands quick and brown on their silver bodies, and they are a school again, swimming, not knowing they are already in the net, already caught in the canoe, eyes dimming in the hot sun, the fisherman standing in the back, he and the wave he chose and the charred tree trunk he hollowed.

"God, it's hot," says my mother. "Let's get out of here."

She has a bundle of fish wrapped in newspaper. I follow her as she pushes through the crowds in the narrow aisles between the stalls. We are in the juju section now. There are monkey paws and skulls and feathers and bright blue and orange and green powders. An old woman leans in the back of her stall fanning herself. She is looking at me. Her eyes are cloudy. She points and beckons. She smiles. There is a flash of gold from her tooth. It shines and shines. I shake my head. My head is a cup. Coins rattle. I hurry after my mother.

"What kept you? I thought I'd lost you."

"Nothing. I was just looking."

"At all those old bones. It gives me the creeps."

"Me too," I say.

She smiles at me. The middles of her eyes are very big and black. Everything stops in my head. "When is Dad coming home?"

"Today. I bet he's home this minute," she says.

When I breathe it's like I was holding my breath for days and I didn't know it.

Facts

I think about the blood on her underwear. I can see it, there when I opened the laundry basket, coffee-colored cotton with a great blot of blood in the crotch staring up at me like it was waiting for me to open the lid, like a spider wrapping its legs around my brain. I can't make it go away. It's a secret. It isn't. She didn't try to hide it. It's lying on top of my father's shirts and socks. Does she want somebody to see? Is she bleeding to death? Why doesn't she tell anybody? Does she pee blood? Why does she pee in her pants? Maybe she couldn't help it. My face feels red and shiny. I wish I didn't see it. It feels weird, like magic, but there must be a reason. I think about Sherlock Holmes. Things look like magic but they never are. There are always reasons. It's always facts and reasons. But I don't know what they are. She might be bleeding to death and not telling anybody because she doesn't want to bother them.

She is alone on the veranda, planting her bottle garden with special long-handled tweezers. The baby plants lie spread out on the newspaper beside her.

"Mother," I say.

She doesn't look up.

"Mum."

First she makes a hole in the earth in the bottom of the giant bottle, then she puts the plant she has chosen, which has purple fleshy leaves, between the tips of the tweezers and she lowers it down so its roots go in the hole. Then she uses the tips of the tweezers to push dirt in around the roots so it stands up. Next she picks a fern with tiny leaves like hair.

"Mum, do you pee blood?"

"No, of course not."

Her eyebrows are joined in the middle now. She's trying to get the fern to stand up. I decide to risk it.

"Why do you bleed then?"

"What are you talking about?"

"Are you bleeding to death? Down there."

"No, silly, of course not."

"Why then?"

"Why what?"

One of the arms of the fern breaks off. "Damnation." She brings it back out with the tweezers and she looks at me. "Ask me no questions and I'll tell you no lies."

"Please. Are you?"

"No," she says. "It's just the curse. Once a month women bleed."

"All women?"

"Yes."

"All at the same time?"

"No, of course not."

"Well why?"

"It's so you can have babies. You will too when you're older."

"I don't want babies. Anyway, why?"

"Because that's how it is. That's how God made it."

"But why?"

"That's enough," she says.

It's no use. She looks at the bottle with her head tipped sideways. The bottle is huge and round like a giant eyeball. I stare at her. All the women in the world bleed every month. It doesn't make sense. I'm going to be thin and tall and read the newspaper. I'm not going to bleed to make babies. Maybe it's not true anyway.

She picks up a little ivy plant and inspects it.

"Why are you doing that?"

"You have to make sure they're healthy."

"No, I mean why are you planting them in a bottle?"

"It's fun, don't you think? A mini-jungle. When you put the cork in you don't have to water it or anything. It's like making a whole little world."

The curse. Who put the curse on her? Who can put a curse on every single woman in the world? If it's magic facts won't work. Facts don't work against magic. There isn't any magic in Sherlock Holmes. People make things look like magic to scare other people away but it isn't real. It's a trick. But who would make all women bleed every month? If there isn't a motive, it's magic. Maybe she is lying. I look at her. Her skin looks like bread that's rising, it's stretching and swelling. I look away quickly. It isn't. It's just the sweat running into my eyes. If she is lying I still don't know why she's bleeding.

Ile-Ibenu

In Old Benin the altars were caked with blood, and naked boys held up the arms of the king. He wore so many bracelets of coral and brass he couldn't lift his own arms. The walls were studded with human skulls and everywhere there were slaves crucified on trees. The soldiers that came and burned the city down vomited at the smell. They were British officers and they called it the City of Blood but the old name was Ile-Ibenu, which means Country of Hatred.

In the museum there is a drawing in ink of the old palace. The display cases are mostly empty except for some leopards and a few bronze heads.

"Ours are better," my mother whispers to my father.

"Ssh," he says.

"Of course," she says, "the best are in London. The Victoria and Albert has a spectacular collection."

I think how the ground drank all that blood. The Oba now is tall and thin. He wears glasses. He looks like a teacher. I saw my father shake his hand in the newspaper. The balsam flowers I planted came up red, not pink or orange.

Underwater

Some days I want to build a castle, tall and strong, around my brother, set it with bones and teeth. He is standing at the end of a dead tree looking down into the pool. The tree leans out over the water. The water is dark green and shiny. His eyes are screwed up as if he is trying to see down into the underneath of the water. The Nigerian boys are lined up at the beginning of the tree. They are laughing and pushing each other. They will just run down it and jump. He looks like a small brown heron waiting for fish. When he dives he keeps his arms spread out like a bird. He cuts into the water without a splash. The boys hit the pond like an explosion of rain, shattering the surface, rocking me where I lie.

Bill comes up beside my mother on the other side. "That was a beautiful dive, darling," she says. I can't hear her but I see her lips moving.

The forest lies down again on the water. I think about monkeys and the crimson butterflies we saw climbing the trail. They were bigger than my hand. I think about one landing on the reflection of a tree by mistake, and how I would slide my hand under, how glad its feet would be to find my finger and then I'd lift my hand into the air and the butterfly would stay and dry its giant wings and I could see up close the pattern like shadows of blue on the crimson.

We couldn't swim in the river because of Belharzia, which lives in river snails and becomes a worm that crawls out through your eye and makes you blind. But we can swim in this pond, which is too high up for the snails.

School starts in four days. Dad has another three weeks of duty in Benin. I wonder if he will come back here alone and swim from end to end making the grasses at the edge shiver and whisper. I think about Lagos and Bill and Christine and school but I don't think about Mum. Her eyes looked funny this morning.

I fill my lungs with air until they push on my bones and then I duck under the water. I swim with long slow strokes. The light in the water is pale green. I can't see far in front of me. My arms pull me through the water. My feet push. The water slides all over me and everything is slow. I let bubbles come out of my mouth. They tickle my cheeks. I think about amber and flies that got stuck in it and how they moved slower and slower as the amber hardened around them. I see myself swimming forever underwater and then I see the whole pond, my father with one arm stretching into the water as the other arm comes out, the boys with their arms and legs folded as if they are sitting, dropping down through the air and the water, my brother with his arms still spread wide and his head thrown back, hanging upside down in the green light, my mother floating on her back, her belly and breasts sticking out of the hard water. My lungs are hurting. I let out all the air that is left and I keep swimming. My head feels light and far away. My body is choking. It is a hard hurting, like someone knocking on my chest. I want to go longer, longer but my legs kick me out into air and I crouch gasping at the edge.

"I wondered where you'd gone," says my mother's voice.

I must have swum right under her.

"It's time for us to go."

I close my eyes. Everything is crimson and black and blue, is opening its wings and shutting them. I am lying in the middle. We are flying away. In the jungle monkeys chatter and worms crawl out of the eyes of children and there are lepers and nuns and Obas. The wings of the butterfly move like breathing. They make the world into shadow then light then shadow then light. I look down. Curled at my feet is my brother. I don't remember his name. I am counting his hairs in the light and the shadow.

Bath

"This is as bad as when you worked in bloody Birmingham all week."

Dad's face is plain. Nothing is written on it. That's how he looks mostly. I like it. It's like a wind that always blows from the same direction. I can hear the jeep in the driveway. The driver is waiting. My father kisses my mother on her lips. He came all the way to Lagos. Now he's going back to Benin and then he's looking at the killings. He's observing them. The jeep wheels spit gravel at us and Dad holds his hand over his head but he doesn't look back. We go into the dining room. My mother takes six pills instead of four. She takes them one at a time, swallowing loudly.

"When did Dad work in Birmingham?" I know the story but I ask anyway. It's one of the ones Dad sits behind a newspaper for but now he isn't here.

"It was when we came back from Hong Kong. You weren't born yet," she says to Bill. He is making a twirl of ketchup on his egg yolk. It stands up an inch off the plate then he takes his knife and cuts down into it so the yellow spills out across the plate and it has streaks of red in it. "When we came back from Hong Kong Dad left the Foreign Office and went to work in a factory in Birmingham."

"Why did he do that?"

"It was part of the training for working with I.C.I. as a scientist."

I meant why did he leave. I don't ask again. I just want her to tell the story.

"We were living in Warwick. Dad was living in digs in Birmingham all week. We were so poor you ate spinach for a whole year. It was the only thing that would grow in the garden there. We wouldn't have made it if Granny hadn't sent us money, and your aunt Gwyneth used to invite us over once a week for a slap-up meal. She would come and pick us up because Dad took the car. Do you remember the car?"

"It was green with a silver stripe."

"I used to push you everywhere in a red and white push chair. There was a toy shop and you fell in love with the golliwog in the window. Do you remember?"

I think I can see the white spots on the red chair but I'm not sure if it's because she told me about it so many times. I still have Golly. He has a red tailcoat and striped trousers and big, surprised eyes.

"You wanted him so much, that golliwog. He cost half a week's rent but I scrimped and saved for weeks and then I bought him for you. You were my only friend, you and Mrs. Brown downstairs, who used to look after you when I went out. But you had a friend, remember?"

"Andy Pandy Jones," I say. I hate this bit.

"In the garden there was a paddling pool. You played there all summer with Andy Pandy Jones, naked as the day you were born.

People in the other flats were shocked. They were such prudes. You looked so sweet together and we'd say how one day you were going to get married."

Bill says, "Anna's not going to get married."

I say, "You weren't even born yet."

My mother doesn't say anything, she gets up. I wish she would finish the story.

She says, "I'm going to the market."

It is Sunday but I don't say anything. I go to brush my teeth. We have strawberry Mr. Punch toothpaste and the taste sticks to my tongue. I tell my face in the mirror how one rainy Sunday my mother said to my father, "I can't stand this anymore, I didn't marry you to live in a slum," and she showed him the ad in the *Sunday Times* where the Foreign Office was recruiting and so Dad became a diplomat again and we moved to London and the cabbies helped Mum start the car every morning by pushing it down the hill and then we went to Germany and Bill was born.

I wish she had finished the story.

Sunday is Christine's day off so we don't have baths on Sunday but my mother is running one anyway and she tells Bill and me to get in.

"I'm not dirty."

"Yes, you are."

She puts Badedas in the bath and it makes green worms in the bottom and the air smells of chestnuts and then she doesn't have any clothes on either. She smells of gin and the middles of her eyes are big and black. I try to look at Bill but he has his eyes closed and he is humming. She puts her hand in the water and it gets bigger. Her breasts are hanging over the edge of the tub. She touches his thing and wiggles it around. He opens his eyes and sits up straight in the tub but she follows him and she doesn't stop. He says, "Mum, don't, it tickles," but he isn't laughing and his voice is little. I am frozen in the water. Only my eyes can move. I wait for my eyes to go up to the ceiling and when they do she looks far away and little, kneeling on the white floor.

She says, "That's what they do, they put their tassels in you, that's what big boys do." She puts her other hand in the water in between my legs. She pushes in me. She giggles and pushes. She is talking in another language. On the ceiling I know she is talking Welsh. "Dirty," she says then and her hand goes away to the tap and Bill says, "It's too hot" to the water and the way he says hot is crying. I want to make him come to the ceiling but he keeps crying. I can't make him stop. Then she gets up and walks away to the door and walks away and the noise of the water fills the room and the steam so I can't see down but I make my hand go to the tap and then it is quiet except he is crying and sniffing and crying and sniffing and I have to make him stop.

His hair makes a wet mark on the pillow and he has blue under his eyes like a bruise. I sing him the only song I know which is *Brown skin girl stay home and mind baby* which I know my father sang to me, that's what my mother said, and so I feel like him when I sing it.

In the morning Christine wakes us up and Bill begins to cry. "What's the matter?" she says.

He says, "I had a nightmare." She strokes his head and tells him to hurry and get dressed then he'll feel better and then she goes away. I wait until I hear her go downstairs and then I go in the bathroom. The bathtub is full of water. I put my arm in and the water is cold. It is green. I pull the plug out. I wait for all the water to suck down the drain and then I go downstairs too.

My mother is eating grapefruit and drinking Alka Seltzer. She says, "Do you want to go to the pool this morning?" Bill nods his head. Tomorrow there is school. In three weeks Dad will come home.

Mosquito

At one time the mosquito was living with the spirits. He was employed as a domestic. Often he was sent on long journeys to far away places. The Queen of Spirits liked him well, she even gave him a horse. Now she had been pregnant a long time. When it was known her labor was about to begin, she sent the mosquito to the land of the animals to fetch the heifer.

"When he arrived he gave the heifer his message and she quickly dressed and joined the mosquito on his horse. But on the way the mosquito stopped and talked to the heifer. He said, 'If you are given any food or gifts, don't accept them or you'll find yourself in trouble.'

"The heifer was still puzzling about this when the mosquito stopped and tied his horse near a small cave.

"'This way, Miss Heifer,' he said.

"The heifer marveled at the cave. It was unlike any cave she had seen before, it was so clean and brightly lit and the entrance was decorated with flowers. She was greeted by five spirits. Two of these spirits had three heads and three legs each but the other three had eleven legs and no heads. Heifer's head swelled with fear. The spirits rushed her to the Queen, whose labor was just starting. The heifer helped the Queen with her delivery. She washed and powdered the baby, then the Queen handed her an evil-smelling ointment, which she requested the midwife to rub on the baby's face. This ointment enabled anyone on whose face it was rubbed to see beyond the land of the spirits. Such a person then would live in a double world, able to see both ways. He could see what was going on all over the earth.

"The heifer felt an itch on her eyebrow and she scratched it. Immediately she discovered she could see more than she did before. She refused all the gifts the Queen of Spirits offered her.

"On the way home she told the mosquito what had happened.

"'Five years ago the Queen of Spirits gave me my horse, and ever since then I have not been able to return home,' explained the mosquito.

"Then the heifer removed the little bit of ointment that had stuck to her eyebrow and she rubbed it on the mosquito's face. The mosquito was then able to see what the spirits saw, as well as all that he already saw. His new intelligence was recognized then by all the spirits, and in no time he was installed as the King of the Spirits. But there was one condition for the kingship, which was that the King should not feed on anything else but human blood. The mosquito accepted this condition and he received the kingship.

"It is since that time the mosquito has lived only on the blood of humans."

It's inside me, the way a magnet pulls iron filings into a pattern, the story's pulling things into a shape inside, quiet and strange.

Christine says, "It's time to brush your hair." She knows I hate hairbrushes but she does it anyway, pulling my hair tight. In her eyes she's gone away. She's gone to the secret place she goes to in her eyes. She wishes she was plaiting her children's hair, tight and black and bristly, into rows. My chest gets hot and sour. They're the ones she's telling stories, not me. I pull my head away and I run down the hallway, dodging the black tiles.

I run down to the lagoon where the mosquitoes crowd, waiting.

Bill

Bill sits on the floor with his legs around piles of coins. He wears blue shorts with an anchor embroidered on the left leg.

"One pound three and six, one pound three and seven, one pound three and eight."

His face is smooth. Only his left hand moves. He takes pennies, one at a time, from the green shoebox and adds them to his piles. When a pile is twelve pennies high he starts a new one. He is singing almost, his voice moving through the changes.

"One pound four and eleven, one pound five shillings, one pound five and one, one pound five and tuppence."

It's like listening to the rain on the roof, the sound it makes over and over, each drop is different but it doesn't matter, it's all the sound of the rain on the roof, and I am inside, listening. "What are you going to buy?" I know what he will say but I ask anyway.

"Nothing."

"So why are you counting your money?"

"Because."

"I know how much you have anyway. You have two pounds three and tenpence." I feel mean when I say it but he doesn't care.

"One pound seven and six, one pound seven and seven."

"So what are you going to be when you grow up?"

"I'm going to be a merchant banker."

"Why?"

"Because."

"Because, because, because. All you ever say is because."

We are like two birds singing the same notes back and forth. Sometimes I test him. I stand over him, my feet inches from his piles, twitching my toes. "Why?"

"Because."

I sit down again. The rain on the roof even sounds like handfuls of coins thrown down from the sky. "Come on, let's dam the gutters." The last time we did that we forgot to take the dam away and the water made a pool on the front porch. It slid under the door and spread across the living room floor. The skirts of the armchairs all got wet. You can still see the stains like tide marks.

"Two pounds three and sixpence."

The bedroom door opens slowly and my mother comes in.

"Lunchtime," she says. "If you want to come to the PX with me after lunch, put on some decent clothes." Her face is heavy grey like the sky.

"Two pounds three and tenpence." Bill takes the piles of money and puts them back in the box. I watch them tumble sideways, the sixpences and thruppences and pennies jumbled up.

"Old moneybags," says my mother. "You'll keep your poor mother in her old age, won't you?"

He puts the lid back on the box and returns it to the closet. He still looks like he is dreaming a slow happy dream. He shuts the door to the closet. "Mum," he says, "did you ever get drunk?"

I want to suck the words out of the air. It is like something cold and dark came up out of the ground and cracked the air in half. I want to look at her but I can't. I think there won't be anything in her eyes.

"No darling, of course not. Wherever did you get that idea?"

Something slips inside me. I can hear a roaring like a football crowd. Go on, says the roar, go on. I am leaning forward.

"I've seen you drunk," he says.

"You have not." She laughs a small laugh. It hangs like a seagull in the air then slips sideways. "I've been tipsy of course. Everyone gets tipsy now and then."

"I don't."

"You're a child."

I want to say something. I can't. I can't breathe. I'm falling forward.

"Come on," says my mother. "It's time for lunch."

I hear wheels crunching on the gravel.

"Do people act funny when they're tipsy?" Bill asks. His eyes are dark brown.

"That's enough now," says my mother.

"There's Dad." She goes out on the landing. "Hello darling," she calls and she goes down the stairs.

Jeremiah brings in my father's suitcase. Gabriel gives him a gin and tonic and my mother one too. We sit down to eat.

"Darling, I'm so glad you're back safe and sound. I was worried sick. How was it?"

"Nothing to talk about over lunch," he says.

Bill is looking at his plate. "Dad," he says, "how do people act when they get tipsy?"

My father looks at my mother. She is holding a chicken leg and biting into it. "That's enough now," he says.

Bill hums and pours ketchup on his chicken. He is a stranger. I don't know who he is. He rocks in his chair like he always does when he eats chicken or spaghetti.

Secret

I am waiting for Dave and Dave's mom. Caroline and I are sitting beside each other on the bench. All day the secret I learned has been buzzing in my head. Caroline swings her feet and hums. She is humming the "Battle Hymn of the Republic." Sometimes she sings a little bit. She sings "Mine eyes have seen the glory," and then she goes back to humming. She is in the smart half of fourth grade with me. Dave is in the other half.

"If there was a war, what would you be?" I feel like my mother making conversation.

"I'd be a nurse."

"You'd sew arms and legs back on?"

"I'm not afraid of blood." Caroline looks sternly at her feet. Her socks are very white. They are always very white. "And I'd write my husband a letter every night."

"And what would he do?"

"He'd fight for his country, of course."

For a moment I think, which country? As if she heard my thought she begins to hum again. She finishes the "Battle Hymn" and then she begins on *Home, home on the range*. When she has finished she says, "In America everyone is free."

I wonder if that is what they talk about in the kitchen, her and her mom. Dave says they spend hours in the kitchen together. Dave is two minutes older. She sits down beside me. Jerry kicks rocks in front of us.

Caroline says, "You'll wear out your new sneakers." She sounds very tired.

Dave says, "Aw, leave him alone."

I look at my knees and Dave's and Caroline's. The sun cuts a ribbon across them. Mine are different, redder.

The sun has gone away and it is thundering. We get in the back of the station wagon except Caroline, who sits in front. It begins to rain. The rain hits the roof and runs down the windows. The windscreen wipers go shh shh and people ride by on bicycles with newspapers over their heads. I feel sleepy and sad. It is like being in a tent and being dry but it is somebody else's tent. The secret I know feels like a mosquito. It shouldn't be there. I shouldn't know it. It is their secret. They know it together.

After we have drunk milk and eaten chocolate chip cookies Dave and I go up to her room and shut the door. She sits down on the bed but I stand by the window. "Is your father really a diplomat?" I ask.

"Sure he is." She sounds surprised.

"He's really the third secretary in the embassy?"

"Yeah, he really is." Her voice sounds annoyed. She doesn't want me to know either. I look at the thick grey rain and then I watch one drop dodge down the glass. I don't want to know anymore. I wish I hadn't heard my mother say it. When you know something you can't make it go away. Just knowing it makes things different.

"What are you talking about?"

Suddenly I know she doesn't know and I am even lonelier. Secrets are lonely. I think that and it makes my throat hurt. If I tell her, she'll have a secret she shouldn't know and she'll always know it. And if I don't I'll have it alone. Maybe she really knows anyway. I can feel her eyes looking at me. When I turn around she makes the secret sign. I am relieved. I have to tell her now. "Your Dad's in the C.I.A. He's not a diplomat. He's a spy. I heard my mother tell my father that and he said it is a secret and she shouldn't ever say it again." I look at Dave then. She is looking at me. I can't tell what's in her eyes.

After a long time she says, "It's not true. He would have told us."

I didn't think about how she wouldn't believe me. "Perhaps he's not allowed to."

"He goes to work every morning just like your father does. Is your father a spy?"

"No."

"Well then, he shouldn't spy on mine."

I nod. Something is tearing inside me. "Maybe he got it wrong," I say.

"No maybe," says Dave. "He's wrong."

"Yeah," I say, "yeah. I guess he got the wrong person." Inside my stomach all the secrets are shaking around like gravel. I can't see them but I know they are there. "Forget it," I say but I know she won't.

Belching

"Mum, how do you belch like that?"

We are sitting on the veranda having tea. The Harmattan wind is blowing. I am drawing spirals in the film of sand on the glass tabletop. The sand has blown all the way from the Sahara.

"I can do it whenever I want." She pauses then does three fat gurgling ones in a row. Bill giggles so hard he spills his tea on his leg. His whole body giggles. It keeps going even when his face is serious again.

"I want to learn how to do that," he says.

"You know how I learnt?" says my mother. She pours more tea. "After my father died, Granny and I went to live in Wales, in Anglesey, with my grandfather, Granny's father." She's never told this story before. "Granny was the oldest and Aunt Gwyneth was the youngest. In between he had five sons. He was a little man, about five foot three, and all his sons were over six foot tall. He used to run after them with a big stick when he wanted to beat them and they always let him even though they could have lifted him off the ground with one hand."

Her voice is getting tight. I look at her and her eyes are small and empty. All the hairs on my arms and legs stand up. It's like a cold wind all over my skin.

"I was three when we went there and I'd never spoken a word of Welsh in my life but he wouldn't have English spoken in the house. He wouldn't even let Granny and me talk to each other in English. We left there when I was six. Gwyneth was seventeen and she begged Granny to take her too. She said the old bugger couldn't keep his hands off her."

She isn't talking to us anymore. I look at my watch. It says quarter to six but I say, "It's six o'clock."

My mother says, "Ask Gabriel to make me a gin and tonic." She says, "He died a nasty lonely death. The only one left with him in that house at the end was the housekeeper and he told her never to come in his room. When she hadn't seen him for three weeks they broke the door down. He was dead on the bed, his arms around a rifle. The room was knee high in empty whisky bottles."

I go to the loo and lock the door. My pee is burning hot. It stings but I listen to it hit the water. It lasts for a long time and when it stops I can breathe again.

On the veranda Bill is drinking Fanta. It is a sharp orange like the heads of the lizards and so sweet it hurts my throat. He says, "Mum, how did you learn to belch?"

I say, "Mum, can I taste your drink?"

I already have my hand around her glass so when she says, "You're too young," I do it anyway.

It makes my whole mouth wrinkle. "Yuk."

She laughs. "It's an acquired taste."

"I'm never going to acquire it."

“Wait and see.”

“Mum,” says Bill.

“Granny’s brothers taught me. They held me over a tub full of freezing cold water. They said they’d drop me in if I didn’t do it. So I did.”

“But how?”

I want him to shut up. My mother lets the ice cubes rattle back down to the bottom of the glass.

“You swallow air down into your stomach. Gulp it down as if it’s food. You hold it there and then you push it back up.”

Bill fills his cheeks with air and sits very still and then his cheeks empty. Nothing happens.

“I’ll try,” I say. I swallow air like I am frightened and then it comes, a little squeaky belch.

“That’s not very good,” says Bill so I do it again. I can feel the big bulb of air in my stomach and then the muscles squeezing it back up my throat. I open my mouth and it comes out loud and wet sounding.

“That’s it,” says my mother.

After a while Bill gets it too and then we both do it until supper.

“I feel sick.”

“Me too,” says Bill.

“Yes,” says my mother, “it does make you sick if you do it too much.”

Isle of Man

The smell is cream and brown and soft, is things which push up out of the ground at night and grow without leaves, which smell the opposite of green, the underneath of green.

Granny looks in my basket. She touches each smooth cap with her long white finger. She knows which are poisonous, which are safe.

My heart is getting big. I'm happy. This is happy. Everything is a smell. I'm a smell in the grass with the mushrooms in the wind in the morning. My knees are wet. A rabbit is watching me. Only his nose moves. Don't be afraid. The smells make a song that's louder than waves. I lick the dew from a blade of grass. The rabbit bounds away, the tips of his brown ears bobbing up above the grass. It will always be this morning and me kneeling and the sun where it is and ladybirds sleeping in the clefts of grass.

My mouth waters. I smell bacon frying, salty and smoky and fat. It's like another bird joining in the song. A cuckoo that squeezes the others out of their nests, nudges their eggs to the edge, fat cuckoo sitting in a robin's nest, all the robin's blue eggs in pieces on the ground. No, it's just another smell song. The sun puts his hand on my back, I can feel his fingers in my hair. When I look up there is a mountain where there was only blue mist before. Where the sun touches, the mountain is purple. In the shadows it is dark blue. It looks like another island floating just above this one.

The air shimmers over the frying pan. The blanket is warm and scratchy on my legs.

"Who's for fried bread?" says my father. He lays two slices of bread in the dark brown juices of the mushrooms and the fat hisses. I take the purple-grey plastic plate.

"Can we climb that mountain?"

Granny smiles. "It's beautiful, isn't it?"

I nod my head because my mouth is full of mushrooms. Granny believes in fairies. She reads tea leaves.

When we get back to the house in Castletown it is raining. She says, "I have a present for you." We climb to the attic. It is grey and old, it smells of ginger and mice. Cobwebs cover the only window. You can hear the sound of rain on the roof like the pattering of mouse feet. She lifts the lid of an old brown trunk. The smell of mothballs covers all the other smells. In the top of the trunk is a tray with wool vests and flannel trousers. "Help me with this," she says. We lift out the tray and I see two pith helmets side by side like two ducks nesting. Next to them are instruments in a leather case whose seam has split and a metal tripod folded up. Granny takes out a small round tin and hands it to me. She takes out a book too but she keeps that. We put the tray back in and close the lid. The pink of her scalp shows through her hair. Her hair looks like a dandelion seed. When she looks at me I am quiet inside. I turn the tin around in my hand. I know what it is. The lid is rusted tight but I open it. It is the cooker she showed me before we ever went to Nigeria, the one she took to the Gold Coast. I remember it. I remember how the metal legs fold out to hold the saucepan.

"You can make your own tea and fry your own mushrooms whenever you go on expeditions," Granny says.

I put the lid back on and it looks like an ordinary biscuit tin. Her eyes are shiny. She's given me a secret.

"It was such an adventure," she says, "the two of us, your grandfather and me. Not many women went to Africa in those days. And of course I had to come back when I was going to have your mother."

I know that bit. "My grandfather." The word feels funny in my mouth. My mother has a photograph of him. He's standing in a river, fishing. He's wearing rubber waders up to the tops of his legs. You can't see his face. "How did he die?"

"In the war. He was a pilot. He died in the Battle of Britain. If we'd lost that battle Hitler might have won the war."

It's what my mother says too. "How old were you?"

"Let's see, Anna was five so I was thirty six."

"What year was it?"

"Nineteen forty."

"So Mum was born in nineteen thirty-five?" But if she had me when she was twenty and I was born in nineteen fifty-eight and she said she was three after her father died and that was nineteen forty. It doesn't add up. I look at Granny. Her skin looks like paper you can see through.

"I don't want you to die." I didn't mean to say that.

"I'll go when it's my time. Not before, not after."

I go and sit by her. "Thank you for the stove." She smells of moss. She doesn't lie to me.

White Man's Grave

Granny says,

> Beware and take care of the Bight of Benin,
> Where few come out, though many go in.

My father says, "You make the best kippers I have ever tasted." The whole house smells of buttery smoky fish.

I say, "What's the Bight of Benin?"

"The sea along the coast of Nigeria," says my father, "but it means the land too."

"When I went to the Gold Coast," Granny says, "people called West Africa 'the White Man's Grave.'"

"Where's the Gold Coast?"

"Ghana now. The old hands liked to scare the new ones with stories of blackwater fever and men going mad and men going native. The worst part was the loneliness. Most wives didn't accompany their husbands. Nobody ever took children to West Africa. They stayed at home with their mothers. I was lucky. Your father," she looks at my mother, "your father wasn't service. He was there on contract to build a bridge. About a year after I had you the contract ran out so he came home."

I eat the last flake of yellow fish. I think about the White Man's Grave but all I can see is the giant billboard outside of Lagos airport. It is a picture of a huge black man with white teeth. He is looking straight out at you, holding an enormous glass. Most of the glass is dark brown like his skin but on top is creamy foam which looks like any minute it's going to run down the sides of the glass. Underneath in big red letters it says, *Guinness Gives You Power.*

Granny gets up and leaves the room. Bill mixes the ketchup on his plate with the juice from the kippers then he dips his finger in it. His finger goes from his mouth to the plate to his mouth. He looks as calm as the grandfather clock in the corner. Granny comes back in holding a thin grey book. It is the book she found in the trunk.

"I thought you'd be interested," she says, handing it to my father.

He looks at the spine and then he opens it. "Nineteen twenty five. An official guide, no less."

"We read it cover to cover," says Granny, "trying to find out what we were in for."

My father coughs and holds the book out in front of him. He reads, "*To anyone about to visit West Africa, the first thing to remember is to discount the tales one hears about the coast, whether before the start, or on board the 'monkey-boat,' as the West African liners are euphemistically termed.* Do you know where the word 'posh' comes from?" He is looking at me. I shake my head. "Listen. *If possible, get a cabin on the port side going out, as in that case one has the advantage of the night land breeze from that side along the coast.* Now do you know?" I shake my head. "Port Out Starboard Home. POSH. The posh people got the best cabins."

“Did you?” I ask Granny. She shakes her head.

“Listen to this. *Always wear a wool cummerbund at night, always wear wool next to the skin and put on a big sweater after polo, tennis, and all hard exercise.*”

“No wonder they died like flies,” says my mother. “Can you imagine? Wool next to your skin in that heat.”

“From dawn to about 4:30 pm a sun topi (hat) must be worn.”

Granny says, “Ladies then didn’t run around trying to turn their white skin black. We did everything we could to keep our complexions.”

I never heard her voice like that. It is pointy.

My mother looks as if she is going to cry.

My father says, “It’s all fashion.”

My mother says, “But white legs look so dreadful.”

Granny says, “Ladies didn’t show their legs either.”

She is going to say something else but my father says, “Listen to this. *Examine often your cooking utensils and cooking place. Allow no native ‘chop’ to be cooked in your pots. Throw it away when you find it therein.* Therein! *Do not flog your boys if you can possibly avoid it. Be firm about their mammy-palaver, but be charitable to the native erotic temperament in doing so. Explain everything over and over again, and speak very slowly and clearly.*”

“Well I agree with that,” says my mother, looking at Granny. I think about her African voice. Granny stops looking fierce.

“Yes,” she says. “I remember that: Empty. The. Latrine. Please.”

“What’s a palaver?” I ask my father.

“A fuss. A great to do.”

“What’s mammy-palaver?” I think I know but I want to be sure.

“Never you mind,” says my father.

I know. I wonder if Gabriel or Daniel or Jeremiah palaver over Christine. I wonder what she is doing, right now, this minute.

God

Granny believes in God. He is white and has a beard. She says that isn't true. She says, "God looks like every single person on earth."

"And animal?"

"Animals don't have souls." She looks at me. "At least, they say they don't. But maybe you're right."

I smile thinly. I've been learning how to smile like that from the woman at the shop by the beach. She does it anytime you ask for anything. It is a smile which isn't a smile. "So God could be a Nigerian? And God could be a woman?"

"God is love," says Granny. She picks a daisy and spins it in her fingers. We are sitting in between the red currant bushes at the bottom of the garden.

"So how come nobody ever says, *Our Mother which art in Heaven?*" I think about the picture of God leaning over the world and I make it my mother's face but I don't like that. I make it Granny and then I make it Christine. "How about *the Mother, the Daughter, and the Holy Ghost?*" I don't want to make Granny sad but suddenly there are more and more questions I never thought of. "Are priests and vicars and ministers only men?"

"Yes."

"Why?" I think maybe she will just say "because" but she doesn't.

She says, "Do you remember the Garden of Eden?" I nod. In the book she gave me, Adam and Eve are running around in fig leaves. He has curly blonde hair. Hers is long and straight. "Well, Eve ate the apple first and then she gave it to Adam. Eve was the one who gave in to temptation. She listened to the snake."

"So?"

"So she committed the first sin which is what they call original sin. All women carry the stain of that sin. That's why we can't be ministers. Women are the weaker vessels."

"That's not fair. Just because she did it first." I feel sick. "Why did she do it?"

"Because she wanted to know too much."

Granny looks at me. Her eyes are saying, 'Like you,' but she's not cross. I want to tell her I'm a boy anyway but I don't. I'm not sure all the time. None of it makes sense. Then I think it's the curse, it's the same thing, but that doesn't make sense either unless maybe the curse is the punishment for eating the apple.

"That's why," Granny says, "when a woman gets married she agrees to be guided by her husband."

"What if she doesn't get married?"

"All women get married."

"What about nuns?"

"Nuns marry God."

"What if God is a woman?" I think about Chiaku and Adagu in Christine's story but I know the priest told Ruth a woman can't marry a woman. Granny doesn't say anything. "What about Aunt Elsie? She didn't get married and she isn't a nun." Aunt Elsie isn't really my aunt. She is Granny's best friend and they read tea leaves together. Aunt Elsie is very tall and she wears trousers even though the neighbors don't like it. She loves pansies. They grow all around her house. When I walk past her house to go to the shop they nod and wink at me. One day I went into her garden. I lay in the grass and looked at their faces. I didn't hear her come out of the house. I started to get up but she put her hand on my head and I lay down again. She lay down in the grass with me.

"They're beautiful, aren't they?"

I nodded. My head felt warm where she put her hand.

"I like the crimson ones best," I said.

She reached out and stroked the petals. "I love them all," she said.

"Sometimes I think they're calling me. They say my name." I don't know why I said that.

She turned and looked at me. Her eyes were quiet and green. "Do you hear them anywhere else?"

"Down by the stream."

Her eyes looked all over me but I wasn't afraid. "You're your grandmother's granddaughter alright," she said and she smiled so her face wrinkled like a turtle. "Come for a walk with me one day, if your mother will let you." Her eyes went grey.

"Yes," I said, "yes please. Now I have to go and buy some butter."

"Come again whenever you want."

When I shut the gate she was still lying on the grass looking at the pansies so I didn't say goodbye.

Why can't I go for a walk with Aunt Elsie?"

Granny is making a daisy chain. She makes the best daisy chains. They never fall apart.

"You have to obey your mother."

"Mum doesn't like her. Is it because she didn't get married? Or is it because she can hear the little people?" I want to tell her that I'm not going to get married either but I don't.

She says, "It wasn't easy for your mother, growing up without a father, being an only child. You're very important to her."

Something twists inside me. I say, "Aunt Gwyneth's husband died, but she got married again."

Granny looks at me. "I suppose I just didn't want to," she says slowly. Then she hangs the daisy chain around my neck. "There," she says. "You can be queen of the fairies for a day." She gets up and goes inside.

I lie and look at the grass through one eye and then through the other, with my left eye the grass is bright emerald green. With my right eye it is browner. I think, now I don't know what color it really is. Everything is like that: the house, the beech tree, the rhubarb patch. I lie on my back and look at the sun through a cluster of currants. They shine like little red eyes.

Home

It's so lovely to be home," says my mother. She kisses Granny on her cheek.

"It's lovely to have you," Granny says.

I am sitting on the trunk under the stairs. The kitchen door is open and I can see through the crack where the hinges are. I can only see a long thin piece of Granny but I saw my mother's lips kiss her cheek. Granny's arm goes up and down. She is making sponge cake. I can smell pears stewing. The smell lies on top of the smell of the trunk. Inside are all my mother's old toys. "Home." It feels funny. "Home." I wonder what my mother looked like when she was a child. I never thought of that before. I can make her body small but her face always comes and sits on top of it like a big crow on a fence post. I want to scare it away and see what she looked like then but I can't. My mother has a picture of Granny when she was younger. She doesn't look anything like she used to. She used to have a long thin horsy face and black hair but now she has cheeks like apples and her hair is silver. Granny is my mother's mother and this is her home. It makes my eyes hurt.

I want something, I want this to be my home too. The Isle of Man. We have home leave and home postings. When we have home leave we come to the Isle of Man. When we get a home posting we will go to England and live there until we get another posting. I'm English so England is where my home is. Now a voice in my head is singing *Home, home on the range where the buffalo roam* and I am singing in American. *Home is where the heart is,* says another voice. Ma's voice. *It's lovely to be home.* My mother's voice is hungry. The sponge cake is baking and then it's like Granny unraveling my old cardigan. She pulled and the wool came loose, leaving little bare knots and then they came loose, one after another, from left to right then right to left, going up, like unwriting, the little knots slipping out of themselves one after another. I put two fingers on my wrist and I close my eyes. Tunk, tunk, tunk, tunk, tunk. I don't listen to anything else. My heart looks like a sea anemone, one of the plump dark red ones that hide in rock pools on the beach. It opens and closes. When the anemone is open, a clown fish swims in between the tentacles. It doesn't get stung. It eats all the food the anemone doesn't want and in return it keeps the anemone clean. In the book the clown fish has bright yellow stripes. It swims among the coral reefs. The water is blue and sunny. If other fish come near, the clown fish hides in the anemone's tentacles.

The anemone opens wider and wider. She's a spider now with jewels in her belly. She's looking at me. "Home," I say, "home." She doesn't move. I don't want her to. The light on her belly will unravel into dark. Everything will get further and further apart. I watch and watch her. I can't blink. She is in the center, her eight legs touching the threads that hold it all together. She is quiet, resting, she doesn't know everything is going further apart. All of it is happening but you can't see, like the moonflower opening, only the spider maybe can feel it in her feet. She sits there in the middle, waiting for something, a commotion in the web, something trapped and struggling she'll seize and bind in her silk, carry back to her nest, mend the web where it tore. She has to keep waiting, listening with her feet.

"Anna, come and have some cake with us." Granny's voice is sweet and grainy like the smell of the pears stewing. "Bring the snakes and ladders board. It's in the trunk."

I look away from the spider, look back. She is still there. I don't know if anybody else knows what would happen if she went away. I open the trunk. It smells of Africa. It was made in Africa before my mother was ever born. In it there are toys, my mother's when she was younger than me. I think the trunk doesn't have any bottom, it goes down in the earth, a black hole smelling of soil.

Magnifying glass

I take my magnifying glass up the mountain. The train is small and full of women in pale dresses with huge arms and legs, and men with great round bellies and veiny noses, and children with skinny white legs. At the top, which isn't really the top, we walk until we can't see many people but we don't walk very far because of Granny.

"How about here?" says my father and he puts down the basket. I put down the rug and keep walking. My feet follow rabbits' paths through the heather. Their hard round droppings are warm from the sun. They smell sweet. I put my cheek on the ground and look through the stalks of the heather. If I were as small as a mouse, it would be a jungle. A bumblebee grips a stem of heather, pulling it down with his weight until it almost touches the ground. His sting is as long as a harpoon. He inches along the stem to the flower, tries to push his giant head inside the tiny bell and falls off the stem.

I find a piece of newspaper and put it in my pocket. A big white rock stands out above the heather. I know which way north is now because that's the side the moss is growing on. The rock is quartz. When I look at the moss through my magnifying glass, it is another jungle and red spiders live in it. The leaves of this jungle are like giant ferns. I crumple the piece of newspaper and put it on the rock, then I hold the magnifying glass between the sun and the paper so it makes a hard spot of light. I hold it like that until the spot goes brown and then black, then the paper curls up on itself and begins to burn. I can't see the flames in the sun but I can see the red rim around the hole getting wider.

"Anna." It's my father's voice. He has been calling for a while. I poke the ashes with a twig and they are all dead. I run back down the path, my feet landing perfectly, one in front of the other, in the narrow channel. The kettle is whistling on the primus. Everyone is sitting on the rug eating chicken legs.

"What were you up to?" asks my father.

"I made a fire how you showed me." He gave me the magnifying glass. It is a good one, heavy glass with a metal band around it and a metal handle. "I made sure it was out," I say, before my mother can open her mouth. "It works," I say, "it really works." My father smiles. I bite into a tomato and the seeds slide down my fingers and fall onto my leg. I lick them off. My leg is brown and salty.

"That's what I said when I made my first radio."

I stop eating. He never tells stories.

"How old were you?" I ask because he isn't saying anything.

"I must have been about fourteen. It was the end of the war."

"How did you make a radio?"

"You take a needle and run it over the surface of a slice of quartz crystal until you find the place where you can pick up a signal, and then you amplify it. That's how the first radios were made."

"And you made one and it worked?"

"I won first prize in a national competition for ham radio operators. I talked to people all over the country and in Europe too. I don't suppose Ma and Pop saw me for more than breakfast and dinner from when I was fourteen till I went away to do my national service.

I think about him in a dark room, bent over a crystal which glows a little, listening to the crackle of foreign voices. It is late at night. His face is very smooth and serious. Sometimes the signals are in code. Downstairs, Ma and Grandpop are sitting opposite each other. I can see the whole house like it is a doll's house with one wall taken off. Grandpop is looking at Ma with his pale blue eyes. Upstairs in the dark my father isn't looking at anything. His head is tilted to one side. He is listening.

"Will you show me how to make one?"

My mother says, "Look at this view. Isn't it beautiful?"

"Yes," says my father. "Yes it is."

I pick up the magnifying glass and look at my leg. The skin has big holes in it. I look at the rug. I hold the glass so the sun points at the rug.

"Hey," says my father, "what are you trying to do?"

I shrug and aim the glass at my leg again.

Aunt Elsie

I have to see Aunt Elsie again. I fetch my bucket and spade.

"Mum," I say, "I want to go and dig bait on the beach."

"Wait until we've finished breakfast and we'll go with you."

"But they're better early in the morning. I'll be careful crossing the road. Dad promised I could go fishing this evening."

She looks at my father who nods. "Alright, but stay near the pier."

"O.K." I am gone before she can say anything else. The pavement feels long and grey under my feet. The air is thick from the brewery. Under the malt smell is the seaweed and tar smell of the harbor. The low stonewalls and picket fences of the front gardens look as if someone dipped a brush in light and painted around them. The houses are little and pale pink and green and blue. Mostly the curtains are open but nobody is out on the street except the milkman. He drives a blue and white electric van. It has three wheels and it hums as it goes from door to door. On the doorsteps, sparrows peck through the silver tops of the milk bottles and drink the cream.

I look in each garden as I walk. I don't look ahead. I see roses and hollyhocks and foxgloves and giant blue and pink hydrangea bushes. I see gnomes with fishing rods and red and white spotted mushrooms and stone bridges with pink and green fairies sitting on them. And then I see the pansies. There is a big black cat sitting in the middle of them. He blinks. I lean on the fence. Most of the pansies are smiling and nodding but some of the dark purple ones and the crimson ones with black in the middle and no yellow look sad. I want to stroke them but I am afraid it will hurt them, like touching a butterfly's wing.

The cat looks at the window. Aunt Elsie is standing there watching me. In front of my eyes I see a thought. "I want Aunt Elsie to be my mother." I read it before I knew what it said. Aunt Elsie is smiling and nodding. I keep looking at her until I am on the step and she is standing in the doorway. I pick up the bottle of milk and hand it to her. The top is pecked through.

"That cat," she says, and she blinks just like the cat. The grandfather clock in the hallway chimes eight o'clock. She is wearing trousers with the zip up the front. They are black and baggy. At the bottom her feet are very small in black boots which lace up above her ankles. She is wearing a bright blue cardigan the same color as the one Granny knitted for Bill.

In the kitchen she says, "Would you like a cup of tea?" I nod. "You don't have time to go for a walk, do you?"

I shake my head. I am glad she knows I can't. Out of the window I can see a pear tree and a quince tree and lots of gooseberries. I move my hand into the square of sunlight on the table. "Did Granny knit your cardigan?"

"Yes." When she smiles, everything in her face moves. She is as wrinkled as a dried apple. A butterfly flies through the window and lands on the geranium. It has eyes on its wings. "Do you know what kind of butterfly that is?"

"A peacock."

"It's called a peacock because peacocks have eyes like that on their tails. Most people think peacock feathers are unlucky. Your grandmother won't have them in the house but I love them." The butterfly is opening and closing its wings so the eyes look like they're opening and closing. "Do you know where butterflies come from?"

"Caterpillars, and then the caterpillars turn into chrysalises and then the butterflies come out." The butterfly flies away.

Aunt Elsie nods. "It's almost like dying when a caterpillar turns into a chrysalis. They lie there in the dark for a long time. They're changing but they don't know what they're becoming. Then one day they start to move. They have to struggle to break out of the chrysalis and they don't know why or what's happening to them, but they do it anyway because something in them knows they have to. It's hard, that blind knowing in the dark, struggling to become something different, knowing that's what you have to be and not knowing what it is."

Her eyes are shining soft green, they are holding me inside them and making me warm like the sunlight on my hand. "That's why butterflies are the special friends of the little people. The little people changed too. Once upon a time they were people like you and me and they lived everywhere but then they weren't allowed anymore. I'm sure they were scared then but they changed anyway. They love the butterflies and the butterflies aren't afraid to listen to them."

"I never thought about butterflies being brave."

"I suppose it's brave," she says, "but in a way they just do what they have to. Perhaps some of them give up and stay in the chrysalis because it's too frightening. But then in there in the dark they die, and that's frightening too."

I look in my teacup. I wonder how she reads the leaves. I know I should go but I don't want to. The clock strikes quarter to nine.

"Shall I read your tea leaves?"

It isn't scary, the way she can see inside. "Yes. Please."

She takes the teacup and everything is still. I don't move even though my foot has pins and needles. Her eyes go dark. I want to cry. After a long time she looks at me. Her eyes are dark green like shadows in the woods. "You're a child." She is angry. "I shouldn't have tried to read your leaves." Her voice is softer. She isn't angry with me. There is a knock on the front door, then another one. She gets up and walks down the hall. I stand up too and pick up my bucket and spade and hold them in front of me. "Hello Mrs. Stevenson, are you looking for Anna?"

"Of course I am." My mother's voice is thin. Aunt Elsie steps aside and I walk past her. "I told you never to come here," my mother says. I walk down the steps. "I told her never to come here." She walks down the steps behind me. I don't hear the door close but I can't look back. I walk in front of my mother. I make my back stiff and tall. Granny is waiting a few doors down. She didn't come with my mother to Aunt Elsie's. She doesn't say anything now either. Nobody does all the way back to the house.

In the kitchen my father is fixing a fishing reel. I sit down and my mother and Granny do too. Bill is lying on his stomach under the red currant bushes. I have to make sure my mother can't see the thought I had. I put it in a box in my head with the things Aunt Elsie said.

"What did she say to you?"

"Nothing." My father doesn't look up. "She told me about how to catch mackerel. She told me lug worms are the best kind of bait and I should dig for them at low tide where the sand is still wet. She told me how to catch conger eels too and how you have to use a special kind of line which is very strong because they're big and mean. Sometimes they're ten feet long. You don't use worms for them, you use a lure and you jiggle it so you trick them and they think it's a fish.

My father begins winding the line onto the reel.

"Why did you go there? Why did you lie to me?"

I can't think of anything else to say. I watch the line going round and round.

"She's an old witch. I won't have her getting her claws into my child." I can feel her looking at Granny. "She's a bloody queer." Granny stands up and walks out of the room. The door closes softly. My mother's hands are fists on the table. "I won't have it."

My father puts the reel down. "Come on now darling," he says. "Let's go for a walk."

Fishing

The sea is a long way down and moving. Bill sits, huddled over his rod, his legs sticking through the railings. He looks old. I wonder if he is sleeping. All the light in the sky is lavender grey. The clouds are like a thin quilt. At the edge they are pulling away in little pieces in the same direction the sea is pulling away from the shore. The pull is so strong on my line it is as if I am standing in the water, the tide sucking the sand out from under my feet, the water making whirlpools in front of my shins.

"A mackerel sky," says my father. "That's what they call this cloud formation."

He is fishing for conger eels with a thick brown cord wrapped around a slab of cork. Granny gave me a fishing rod for my birthday, which hasn't happened yet, and she gave Bill one too though his birthday was two months ago. Mine is blue. His is white. Under the water in the dark all the fish are going away from the shore. They are pointing in the same direction as the wind. I see them like little silver stitches in the black water. Only the eels stay, coiled in caves at the foot of the pier. They have huge jaws and thin teeth. Their teeth glow in the dark like the numbers I've written down in the book I bought, an arithmetic book with squares for each number. 1958 – 20 = 1938 1940 – 5 = 1935 1935 + 20 = 1955 1940 – 3 = 1937 1937 + 20 = 1957. I showed my father the sums. He said, "That's right. That's right. That's right," and at the bottom he put a big tick. All the times she said she was twenty when she had me, he knew she was lying. If the sums are right, if they are really right. They add up and subtract in my head over and over. I look down at the water. I think about the hook, hanging by itself in the dark, waiting. Then the float is gone. The reel starts going around and around.

"You've got one," my father says, his voice so quiet he is almost whispering. "Start playing it in." The fish pulls and pulls. The tip of the rod bends over the railing but it doesn't break. When the fish is flapping in the air he reaches over and grabs it. It is blue and silver and green, twisting on the pier. He picks up the stone he brought from the beach and he hits it on the head. Its eye goes red.

He holds it by the tail. "A mackerel," he says. "Good catch." He lays it down on a sheet of newspaper. Behind it the lights of the town are like a net thrown over the houses. It lies there alone on the square of newspaper in the middle of the pier. The colors are sucking out of it.

The top fin is spiny in my palm. I take the knife in my right hand and I draw it down the pale skin of the belly. It doesn't go in. I push harder. I slice from the mouth down to the tail. Inside are the organs. I see them together, dark brown, nestled like fledglings. I scoop them out, tearing the membrane like a spider's web. The heart is small and firm between my fingers. It is perfect. I don't think anymore. I put it in my mouth and I swallow it like a pill. My fingers are bloody. I turn on the tap and wash the rest of the guts out into the sink. I wash the fish until its flesh is grey.

“Here,” says Granny.

The kitchen smells of burning butter. The mackerel skin is gold and crisp. It lies in the middle of the table. Its eyes are blind white.

My mother is holding a piece of the mackerel in her fingers. She is moving it from the plate to her mouth. My heart is beating very fast. “Mum. How old are you?”

“Young enough to have my teeth, old enough to count them.” She licks her fingers. “You don’t ask women their age. It’s rude.”

“No but really.”

“Anna,” says my father.

Airplane

Everybody except two nuns is carrying red, white and blue shopping bags. The bags are heavy, they strain at the little plastic handles. On the sides I read *Heathrow International Airport Duty-Free Lounge.*

"What did you get?" Bill stands up and looks in the bags. "Gin or vodka. Mmm, I bet it's Beefeater gin. One of brandy, one of whisky. Why didn't you get Southern Comfort?"

My mother says, "Yuk. Too sweet."

My father laughs. "You're a regular barman. What do you know about Southern Comfort?"

Bill shrugs and sits down again. He is taking apart a Lego jet plane piece by piece.

"What is Southern Comfort?" I ask, looking at him.

My father says, "It's the opposite of Mother's ruin."

"What's Mother's ruin?"

"Gin."

"Why do they call it that?"

"Because in the nineteenth century it was very cheap and a lot of women drank it."

"Is it very cheap now?"

"No, not at all."

"The damned plane is late," says my mother.

In my head the White Man's Grave and Mother's ruin begin to do a dance. "Did Granny drink gin?"

"No," says my mother, "only champagne. For years she drank a half bottle every morning."

I see her in her hammock in the compound with the lions roaring, sipping champagne. The image is fuzzy, as if I am looking through mosquito netting. "But she doesn't do that anymore?"

"No, she stopped a few years ago."

"Why?"

"The doctor told her to. She was ill."

We are all silent, looking at the big black board overhead. White letters click over, each in its special slot. B.U.E. "Buenos Aires," I say. There is Madrid and Corfu and Tunis and Bombay and Pretoria.

"I think I'll go to Tunis," says my mother, "that dry desert air."

"I'll go to Buenos Aires," I say, "and climb the Andes."

"I'll go to Pretoria and find diamonds."

I look at Bill. I think, I don't know you at all. "How do you know diamonds come from Pretoria?"

"Lagos," says my father. "Here we go." The voice coming out of the loudspeaker is excited and too crackly to understand. "Gate twenty-seven," says my father.

London gets smaller and smaller. It's like looking at a fingerprint or a crew cut, the way the rows of houses curl around each other. My tongue pokes into the sharp middle of the lemon drop my mother gave me to suck. England, I think, England. Home. I yawn and hold my nose and blow down it but my ears won't pop. I press my face against the window. I want to open it. I want to break it, to feel the cold sky come rushing in on my face. I think, it's like being in a diving bell in the air. But my mother is sitting next to me. I can smell her sticky sour sweet smell everywhere. She leans over me to look out and I feel a thick wave coming up my throat. I grab for the sick bag but nothing happens.

"Oh God," says my mother, "don't be sick."

I shake my head. The stewardess is standing up at the end of the aisle. She has pointy black shoes with thin heels. Her fingernails are red and sharp. She points at the emergency exits. She holds her arms in the air pointing at them for a long time. Then she puts on an orange life vest. When she pulls a button it swells up so she has an enormous orange bosom. Tits. I hear Dave's voice in my head. Orange tits. She pulls out a long tube from over somebody's seat and she holds it against her mouth, then she fastens it to her face. I wonder what else she will put on but she doesn't. She takes off the mask and the life jacket and she goes away. A voice says, "You may unfasten your seat belts now."

When the drinks cart comes around my mother says, "I shouldn't. It always gives me a headache. But I'll have a gin and tonic please."

"Why do they wear shoes like that?"

"Because the airline wants its stewardesses to look beautiful."

"So they have to wear them? Like uniform?"

"Not exactly. They want to."

"Why?"

"It makes them look taller and slimmer."

"Do you wear shoes like that?"

"You know I do."

"Do they hurt?"

“Not once you get used to them. Now it’s not comfortable for me to wear flat shoes.”

“What if you were wrecked on a desert island and didn’t have any shoes?”

“Don’t be daft,” says my mother. “Why don’t you do your jigsaw?” She takes it out of the bag between her feet and puts it on my knees, then she pulls the magazine out of the back of the seat in front of her.

I look out of the window. I wish Dad was sitting next to me but he is sitting next to Bill. Bill is asleep with his cheek squished up against the glass. I half close my eyes so the clouds are like giant white birds flying underneath us. I can’t make the bitter smell go out of my nose, even though my mother finished her drink a long time ago. I let myself out of the window and I fly on the bird’s back. It is soft like a bed. I keep sinking into it so I can’t breathe and then the plane comes lower and lower on top of me and all the air smells of gin. I try to push the plane away but it is soft too and my hands sink into it and it keeps getting bigger and it is hairy on its belly and I am drowning in a smell that is my mother’s smell.

I know it is her smell and I pull my body in around me tighter and tighter and then the wave comes again and again, thick and wet on my belly.

“Here,” says my mother’s voice, “here. Use this. For goodness’ sake, use the bag.”

I throw up again into the bag. I don’t want to open my eyes.

“Come with me,” says another voice. It is the stewardess. My belly and my legs are cold and wet. I can’t make my eyes open.

“Come on, darling,” says my mother. She says, “She’s never been airsick before.”

“Do you have any clean clothes for her?”

“Yes.”

I can hear her rummaging under the seat. I open my eyes. The stewardess is smiling at me. "I'm dirty." My voice is little. I begin to cry. "I'm dirty." She doesn't stop smiling.

My mother gives the stewardess my green dress. "Thank you."

"All part of the job," says the stewardess.

I look at her feet all the way to the bathroom. I smell. She is holding the bag in front of her. I can't stop crying but I don't make any noise. The water keeps leaking out of my eyes and my nose. Her heels make little dents in the carpet.

In the bathroom she tells me to stand on the toilet, otherwise there won't be room for us. She unbuttons my cardigan and takes it off and she puts my hands over my head then she pulls the dress up over my head and my hands. I don't move. She wets a paper towel and wipes my stomach and my legs. She wipes them carefully. Her hand moves very slowly. I don't think about anything. She pulls the clean dress down over my head. "What a pretty dress," she says. "Did your mother make that for you?"

I don't say anything. She puts my arms down by my side, wets another towel and wipes my face. It is cold. "There," she says, "good as new." She washes her hands. Her nails are scarlet against the silver basin. I don't want to move. She opens the door and lifts me down from the toilet. I stay how she put me. She bends her knees so she is looking in my face. "'It's not bad to be sick," she says. "Look." She turns me so we are looking in the mirror. "You're not dirty anymore."

I look at her face. She has long black eyelashes. She doesn't have any clothes on and her legs are wide apart and her head is thrown back and her mouth is open and she has blonde hair down there. She is still wearing her shoes. She is looking at me through eyelashes like long grass. "Come now," she says, "you're all clean and pretty again."

Jigsaw

My eyes are thick and my throat is dry. I'm awake. I know where I am. My mother's seat is leaned back as far as it will go, and her head is leaned back too. Her mouth is open. I can see lipstick on her teeth. She is snoring. I look out of the window: the same white clouds. Perhaps we haven't moved at all. We got stuck. No, they're different. The Isle of Man is slipping further and further behind us under the clouds, Granny and Aunt Elsie and the brewery seaweed smell sliding over the horizon. We must be over the Atlantic by now. I get out the magazine which has all the flight paths drawn in red on the maps like the paths of birds migrating to the same place, year after year, to the same tiny pond, and butterflies too, flying down from Europe to Africa for the winter, they know exactly where they are going, even when they are in the middle of nowhere over the Atlantic they know, they must know they're in the right place. But then I think about what Aunt Elsie said, about how they just do what they have to do and maybe they don't know, they don't remember last year or they weren't born then, but inside they know they have to go and when they're in the middle of the Atlantic there isn't any point in stopping anyway. Maybe the knowing is like a singing, they can't quite catch the words so they keep going, trying to get close enough to hear, and then they're on the other side of the Atlantic already. I don't know if they hear the words then or if they ever do, and if they did, would they stop flying then?

My mother shifts and mutters in her sleep. She is dreaming. I know because her eyelids are flickering. I put away the magazine and take out the jigsaw puzzle. I fold down the little table. The picture on the box is a thatched cottage with hollyhocks and roses and lupines growing in front of it, and an apple tree to the left. I wonder if it would be better to do a jigsaw without seeing the picture first. You could start at the edge and work in. They always put the picture on the box so you know what you are buying. But nobody keeps a jigsaw when it's done. I put the top of the box under the bottom. I try to forget what I've seen. Blind people can do jigsaws. I like to feel the wooden pieces in my hand, the inlets and coves and promontories, each piece like a secret island.

When I only have a hole left in the middle, my mother wakes up. Her eyelids are red and puffy. She yawns. "God, I have a headache," she says. She presses a button and a light goes on over her head. The stewardess comes. She smiles at me. I can feel her smile but I don't look.

"Could I have a glass of water?" My mother gets out two codeine. Then she puts her hand in the box and takes out a piece. "This bit goes there." She puts it in. It is a part of the thatch roof. When the stewardess comes with the water and my mother tips her head back to swallow the pills, I take the piece out and put it back in the box. I try to forget which one it was. My mother stays with her head back and her eyes closed but she is not asleep. I hurry with the puzzle. It is like there is a snake closing in on the gap, I have to keep feeding it pieces, one after another. I am not thinking about anything. The captain's voice says, "We will be landing at Lagos International Airport in approximately twenty minutes. The captain and the crew hope you have enjoyed your flight." I put in the last piece. I'm glad I hurried. I can see the thatched cottage again but it is like looking in a broken mirror. It isn't the same as the picture on the box even though it is the same picture.

"Look," my father says across the aisle. I look out of the window and everything below is green except for the red cuts in the jungle where the roads are.

"Oh that's beautiful," says the stewardess, "what a beautiful home." She is leaning over my mother, looking down at the table. I keep seeing the heels of her shoes sunk in the sand so she can't move. She can't run. "Let me help you," she says, but I slide the puzzle over the edge into the box so it breaks into pieces again. "Oh," she says, "what a pity." I can't look at her. I wish I could. I want to look at her eyes behind the eyelashes. "Shall I help you fasten your seat belt?"

"I can do it," I say and she goes away. Out of the window I see acres and acres of corrugated tin roofs. They touch each other. Their walls are made of cardboard and sacks.

In the harbor there are white and grey ships with red funnels and then there is the runway and men like ants running everywhere. The wheels touch the ground and the whole plane shakes. All the Nigerians cheer.

When we get to the door, the stewardess is standing there smiling at each person. "I hope you enjoyed your flight. I hope you enjoyed your flight." She hands my mother a plastic bag and my mother says, "Thank you," and then it is my turn. I take a deep breath and I look up into her face. Her eyes are blue suns, they are shining and shining. "Have fun," she says and she touches my shoulder and my shoulder is warm.

I step out into a wall of thick wet air. The silver steps shine so bright I can't see. I slip. The metal scorches the back of my leg. "Lagos, Lagos, Lagos," I say. I can smell the jungle. I know how the jungle smells, how it is thick and green and brown and sweet and dead. On the runway my mother says, "You might have said thank you." I smell the jungle until it is everywhere in my body. Tomorrow I'll see Dave. I'll be a sailor and a spy.

Recipe

"A toast to Brigadier Banjo." Peg raises her glass. The ice cubes clink.

Brian reaches for the jug on the table. They are drinking Pimms Number One. "Top-up, anyone? The rebel forces came within a hundred miles of Lagos while you were away, you know. It wasn't the noble Nigerian army that drove them back either, it was their own commanding officer. The brave Brigadier decided to turn around and see if he couldn't knock off Ojukwu and seize power himself."

"He got shot for his efforts, cheeky devil," Peg says, holding out her glass.

They are laughing but my father is shaking his head, "It's all-out war now and the Biafrans don't stand a chance."

"What, against an army whose commanders order the troops from their own tribe to go to the rear before any advance? The Easterners are winning the propaganda war, that's for sure. Brave little Biafra."

My father takes a cigarette from the silver box on the table. He taps it three times but he doesn't light it. "It's a recipe," he says, "for tragedy. Gowon will starve them out. What else can he do?"

Peg and my mother shake their heads and then they pick up their drinks. They pick them up at the exact same time. Bits of orange and lemon and mint bob up and down in the brown liquid.

Lines

The lines on her face are roads to the war. They cut the skin and put mud, they put the ground in her blood. Now it's like looking from the air, like the roads cut in the jungle I saw from the plane. She's going back. She has to. I look at the scars. I keep looking at them. She's going to the war. I look at her arms. They are big and strong. She won't die. A bubble in my chest is getting bigger, "Why? Why do you have to go?" It's in the air floating away from my mouth. She looks at me. The middles of her eyes are black. They are mirrors. There are babies in them with bellies like balloons. There are bodies covered in ants. There's a man lying on his back with a hole through his chest. The ground is dark all around him. It's a blood bath. My father's voice. She's wearing her white dress. I want to hold the hem and never let go. Don't go. Don't leave me here. She spins away from me, the white dress unwinding like a bandage. She is naked. She is going. Christine. Christine. I look at the ground again, sticky and crimson. It's the ground she has in her arms. The man lying dead is where she grew yams. It is home. They put home in her blood. "What are you going to do?"

She is walking down the line, the front line, like a tightrope, her arms out on either side, balancing, and nobody is shooting. Everything is quiet. At the other end of the line the Killing Ghost is waiting. Her skin is white as paper. There's no color in her eyes. She smells of dead animals. She is waiting for Christine and Christine is brown and gold and orange and purple. She's hot as the sun. She's shining.

"I have to go," she says.

Twin

A plant with spiky pods grows under the kitchen window. I kneel there. Inside Daniel is reading a recipe in French. My father is coming. He is coming home today. There are holes nothing fits into. I watch ants go in and out of a pine-apple. They have made a tiny round entrance. When they come out, their bodies are shiny.

I break off some pods and I go down to my hut. All this week I carved my twin out of a piece of wood. He is very small because he lives in hiding. He has a name but it is a secret name. I am care-ful never to say or even think it. When I sit in the hut which Michael built, which grows, it is like dreaming. There are stars in the sky which are diamonds. Diamonds fall on my skin. Skin is a snake curled like a pot. In the pot is the twin. Stars fall and be-come sand. Twin lies on sand. The snake ate food and fed the twin. Today the twin must eat its own. I break pods and lay them there. "Eat. Eat. Grow big."

I ate and starved my twin to death. I ate, I drank, I starved my twin. Diamonds are falling. My tears. I cry in the dark "Drink, twin, drink." I lift him, he drinks. "You killed me," he roars and the stars go out in the dark. He is the angry one. "Eat," I say, "eat." I offer him pods. I lift them to his mouth. "Is it good? Is it good?" The sky is raining through the holes where the stars were, the stars are grey, they fall on my face, my hands. I bury my twin in his bed of sand. "Sleep. Sleep." I sing,

> Brown skin girl, stay home and mind baby,
> Brown skin girl, stay home and mind baby,
> For I'm going away on a sailing ship
> And I don't know when I'll be back again,
> So brown skin girl, stay home and mind baby.

When I step outside my eyes go black with the light. My shirt is wet. I look at my hands and they are red. I can't stop looking at them. I hold them out in the rain. The rain can't wash them clean. They're not my hands. My bloody hands. That's my father's voice. This bloody business. This bloody war. My bloody hands.

"Anna," my father calls, "Anna, come and see what I've brought." I can't hide them. He will see. He will know. I walk toward the house. He is standing holding a knobby thing the size of a head, a small head. He takes a knife and splits it open. Inside it is yellow and stringy, small black seeds shine like opposite stars.

"What did you do to your face?" says my mother. "Your hands." My father is laughing. My father is a blind man. "Oh," says my mother, "she found the henna plant."

"Wait till you look in the mirror," he says. "You look like the original savage."

"It stains," says my mother.

"Women use henna to dye their hair, isn't that right, darling? You dyed your face. Scrub all you like, it won't come off for a while."

"Just as well it's the school holidays. You'd never hear the end of it."

"Try this," says my father. "It's called custard apple."

He hands me a slice and I lift it to my mouth. Every time I eat I will see my red hands.

"It's good," says my mother with her mouth full. "It doesn't taste much like custard or apples but it's good."

"Taste it," says my father. It is sticky white and sweet on my tongue.

"Where's Richard?" my mother asks.

"He's taking a shower. It was a long, dirty trip. Hard to tell much even from the air, but the Red Cross man said conditions are terrible on the other side. The soldiers took what harvest there was. The villagers are starving. He doesn't think they can last long."

"How dreadful."

"Yes, in a way. But you know, they can't win, so the sooner they surrender, the less damage there'll be. If only the bloody French don't start sending them aid."

Richard comes down the stairs. He is wearing khaki shorts and a white shirt. His hair is slicked back and shiny.

"Go and shower, darling. Dinner will be ready soon." She turns to Richard, "I expect you're starving," she says, and she smiles.

Prince

"You've done the house up beautifully," says Richard. My father is at the office.

"Thank you," says my mother.

Richard smiles. He taps the side of his leg with his hand over and over. It is like he is reminding himself of something, but maybe he doesn't even know he is doing it. He is a prince. Not the kind that gets to be king, unless twenty people die off in the right order. There is something different about my mother's smile, it stays on her mouth a little bit too long, and her eyes keep following a curve, up to his face then down again.

"Really," he says, leaning over the coffee table with his hands behind his back, "you have a gift." The bronze leopard stares at him.

I am sitting on the stairs looking in between the banisters. It is like watching T.V. I am not hiding but they don't look at me.

"In Hong Kong I started a small business doing interior decorating. It was quite successful actually. I was very young. But then I had Anna and I had to stop. I was only twenty. I just couldn't manage both things. We had a Chinese amah of course, but I was exhausted. It was a pity. I was really doing very well, though I say so myself."

"Well," says Richard, "you've certainly made a beautiful house out of what I'm sure was not very promising material." He is tapping his leg again.

"You should have seen the place when we arrived. Those chairs were covered in thick beige material, the lumpy, scratchy kind. It was like sitting in a bowl of dried-up porridge."

Richard laughs one short laugh, like Red's bark when he is surprised.

"I thought a very pale green would be the most soothing in this climate. I had a local tailor make up the chair covers and the curtains. And of course we had the whole place painted white. It was that dreadful DoE cream. I almost had a fit. Really, I think the designer must have grown up in a council house in Birmingham." She says Birmingham as if she has liquid in her nose. Burbighum. "No idea of living in the tropics. Besides the taste . . ." She pauses. I am getting dizzy watching her eyes. "Too dreadful." She says "too" at the same time as she is breathing out and it lasts a long time.

She sounds more and more like him. He sounds as if he has a very long neck and he doesn't ever want to waste too much breath on a word.

"Look," she says, and her hand lands on his arm. It waits for a moment before it takes off again. Everything is happening slower and slower. "Come and look at the Ibejis." She puts her hand on his elbow and it stays there. They go into the dining room. "Aren't they marvelous?"

"What are they?"

"The Yoruba make one whenever a twin dies. As a child, but they, um, endow them with adult attributes."

"I'll say."

I feel sick. They will touch them.

I stand up and walk down the stairs. My legs are stiff. I walk into the dining room. He is holding one of the Ibejis upside down. His fingers are wrapped around her stomach.

My mother says, "What is it? You look as if you've seen a ghost." I can't make my eyes go away from the upside down Ibeji. I can't make them blink. The air around the figure gets darker and darker and then there are little pricks of light and they are moving like breathing. He turns her right way up and puts her back on the shelf but I can't stop looking at the same place. I hold out my hands straight in front of me. They are red.

"Well," he says, "I think I'll catch the news before dinner."

I know I am still staring. My arms and legs feel like they are carved out of wood. I know I can move but the part of me that knows that is a long way away, watching the part of me that is standing still and staring. "Well," he says. I feel him leave the room. My mother leaves too.

"I'm sorry, I don't know what's got into her lately."

The air is hundreds of dots of light. They move like the sea or somebody breathing. Sometimes they get darker, then lighter again. I wonder if it will ever stop. My mother comes in and shakes my shoulder. "What's the matter with you?" I hear her but my body is wood, it tips from side to side when she shakes me and my eyes don't move. Then my watching part says, "It's time to stop." I don't want to but I let the thought pass over into my arms and legs and my eyes blink.

"What on earth has gotten into you?"

I put my hands in my pockets. I blink again. The light is still moving.

"Well?"

"Nothing."

“What do you mean nothing?”

“I was playing statues.”

“Don’t you ever do that again. Poor Richard. What a weird family he must think we are.”

“It was just me being weird.”

“Yes, and I’m your mother.”

In my mind I promise the Ibejis I will come and see them later.

“Go and put on the strawberry dress and the coral pink ribbons for your hair.”

She knows I hate that dress. It is green and white with little red strawberries all over. She made it herself. She makes all my dresses. She always says, “Oh God, I hate sewing” but she makes them anyway and I hate them.

“It beats me how you can be wearing jeans in this heat.”

I shrug.

“Go on now.”

“Why?”

“Because I told you to. Anyway, Dad doesn’t want to come home from the office sweaty and tired to see you looking like a tramp. He loves you in that dress. Do it just to please him.”

I walk out onto the veranda.

“Where are you going?”

I don’t look at her. I climb up the rope ladder and over the railing and I go into my bedroom.

Story

I am in the growing house with my twin. Dark is pouring through the door. He is asleep. Perhaps he is dead. "I'll tell you a story," I say, "about a little girl, a little little girl who was wearing a red party dress, it was made of velvet and on her legs were thick white tights. She was outside. Inside there were her grandmother and her grandfather and her mother and her father. She could hear her grandfather laughing. He had a big belly and her grandmother had powder on her face and they brought her a sheepdog called Big Ben who was grey and white and curly and he had little red wheels. He was taller than her. He was a present. 'How pretty she is,' they said, 'our first grandchild,' and her grandmother knelt and looked in her eyes and her grandfather took a photograph of them together.

"Outside in the hall she began to unbutton her dress. She pulled it off over her head. She unbuttoned her shoes and slipped them off and she peeled off her tights, one leg at a time, balancing against the wall. She took off her panties and her vest with the pink rose on the front. It was cold here and dark but she wasn't shivering. Inside it would be bright and warm. When she walked in the room she was looking in her grandmother's eyes and she saw her grandmother's eyes go dark and her face go grey but it was too late to get dressed again and she was standing on her grandfather's knee and he was holding her arms and her mother was standing against the fireplace. There wasn't anything in her mother's eyes. The little girl put up her hand to cover her shoulder but she couldn't hide her legs. She was ugly. 'Look at that. Look at those bruises,' said her grandmother.

"It was too late to get dressed again. It was dark in the middle of the light where she was standing and then her grandparents went away in their car and she never saw them again for a long time, and her father went away too. The End."

The twin looks at me, he has one red eye in the middle of his forehead, and he roars. He gets up from his bed of sand and he roars. He is covered in red stains which are blood.

"Go to sleep," I say. I am afraid somebody will hear him. He runs in circles in the sand. "Please," I say, "please stop." Then Christine's face is looking in the door. "Please," I say, "make him stop."

She is smiling. "He is a lion," she says. She doesn't have a body, just a face, and then her face has gone away.

The twin is breathing in the dark and breathing out the dark until the dark is bigger than the hut and bigger than the house and it is a huge wave breaking everything apart. I see my brother carried on the wave and he is crying but I can't reach him. Then I am crying because there isn't anything left, only pale sand with little ripples and some pieces of seaweed and a doll with no arms and my tears fall on the twin and the twin lies down and goes to sleep in the sand.

Observer

"Dad says the war's almost done."

Dave swings her sneakers. They are new and red with blue stars on the ankles.

"He's been watching. He's making sure Christine gets home safe. She's on her way. I told you that."

Dave swings her feet higher in the air. "Your father's spying on the war. He's the spy."

I look at her. I wish I never told her about her father. I think now when she looks at him she's always wondering if he lied. I want to ask her if that's true. She's staring at her toes, at two half moons of unstained rubber.

"He's an observer," I say. "It's different."

Hole

He almost starved to death, poor little chap. They wouldn't let me breastfeed him. In those days they thought it was healthier to bottle feed but Bill didn't think so, did you? You didn't want that crummy bottled milk. You lost so much weight they put you in the incubator. If Dr. Braun hadn't come and seen you, you would have died. He took one look and said, 'We have to get them out of here.' He took you, and Dad got all my stuff and we went scurrying out before anyone could stop us. I've never been so glad to get home. The hospital was furious. I had milk fever because they wouldn't let me feed you, so we fed you Carnation milk and you lapped it up. You got positively pudgy."

Bill scowls but he is pleased. My mother is twirling a yellow paper rose with a green stem between her fingers. Something in my belly turns and turns like bath water sucking down the drain. It's pulling something in my head. The yellow petals are faded and wire is sticking through the green paper.

My mother is looking at me. "You weren't jealous at all. You loved him right away. You wanted to play all the time. I'd come in and find you just standing there looking at him while he was asleep and I'd ask you what you were doing and you'd say you were waiting for him to wake up."

"Granny was there, wasn't she?"

"Yes, she came and looked after you."

Under the apple tree where the swing was, the grass was covered in white petals. And one day a squirrel sat on the sideboard holding a walnut. He sat in a sunbeam and his fur was orange.

These are my memories. She doesn't know them. When she tells stories I don't know if I am remembering what happened really or just what she said when she told the story the last time, but sometimes when I can see a picture in my mind and everything looks big, I think I remember. And sometimes it isn't the kind of thing anybody tells stories about, like when I was on the swing and the wind was blowing my dress out in front of me, big and round, and apple petals were landing on me like butterflies and I heard the car door slam and my father called, "Anna," and I looked at him where he was standing by the gate and the chain of the swing went back and forth across him like a windshield wiper. I know it was when my mother came back from the hospital but I don't remember going to him and I don't remember seeing my brother for the first time. I want to remember. I want to remember for myself. I want to remember everything that ever happened. Then I could tell it in a story and everything would be true. It wouldn't have any holes in it. It would be huge and true and fine and strong, like a parachute made of silk.

My mother is still talking and holding the rose. Her voice is buzzing. She is yellow and black, a bee pushing its head inside the flower. The black stripes are growing and growing.

My mouth is slimy. It's full of spit now but I can't swallow. People are laughing in another room. That's not true. There aren't any people. Only my mother and my brother and my father and

I. My father is reading the newspaper. I go down to the lagoon. I sit under the canna lilies. The flowers are dark red and the leaves have dark red veins. I look at the edge of the lagoon. I think, I am like Daniel. I have a photographic memory. I take a photograph of the pebbles at the edge of the lagoon and I look at it. The pebbles look like bones. Bill nearly starved but the doctor saved him. I starved my twin to death. I ate everything. He couldn't even cry. He sat in a corner and rocked. I can see the walls. They are green, dark bluey green all the way to the floor. I'm making it up. I can't really see. I don't know if I had a twin. The picture isn't really there. I can see me telling Dave. We were sitting in the pawpaw tree and Jenny was listening to the Monkees. I told Dave about my twin. I don't know if it's true. Something in my head is empty. Where I should find pictures it is dark. It isn't just dark and empty, it's a hole that everything is rushing into. It's sucking me in.

I can't hear my heart. The rushing is going on, it's tearing at me, it's pulling my skin. My skin is flapping like spider webs, all torn. I have to see a picture. It will have edges. It will be square. I make the frame in my mind. I see the frame. It is wood. Inside it I see Christine's face. Christine. Christine. But her face is like a slide. I can see through her face and on the other side there are children. They are black. They have huge bellies like they ate too much or they are pregnant but they are starving. If you took a pin they'd pop and only rubbery bits of skin would be left on the ground. They are looking into the eye of the camera. They are Christine's children. Christine is back. Her babies are dead. They died in the war like soldiers. They are looking into the eye of the gun. They were her children and she came back and they are dead and they were children. They got lost in the bush maybe and the jackals ate their bones and Christine called their names, she walked in the bush and she called their names but they didn't come. She left them in the bush where they are dead and in her eyes is the hole which is dark, which is empty, and everything is rushing in, the wind is tearing my skin, I mustn't look in her face anymore. I look in my father's. His mouth is moving. I can't hear what he is saying. His mouth is the hole. The wind is tearing in. Listen. I have to listen. I can hear him. His voice is crackling like the radio. It's coming from a long way away.

He says, "You look glum. Do you want to hear a joke?"

I nod my head.

"It's an old family joke. Perhaps I'd better wait till you're old enough to understand."

"Tell me now."

"Are you old enough?"

"Yes."

"Perhaps you are," he says. "Alright. Why is a mouse when it spins?"

"Why is a mouse when it spins?"

"Yes."

"I don't know."

"Because the higher it gets, the fewer."

"Because the higher it gets, the fewer?"

"Yes."

"I don't get it."

"You don't what?"

"I don't understand it."

"You'll just have to wait till you're old enough then."

"What does it mean?" He shakes his head. He is smiling.

"It won't ever make sense."

"That's what I said," he says, "when Grandpop told me the joke." I stare at him. The black comes rushing out of me at him. It rips his skin away from his bones. Only his eyes are left. They are blue. When he opens his mouth with no lips shit comes pouring out, yellow, brown, green. Shit. Shit. Shit. All I am is ears hearing the wind and the words. I don't have a body any more. I don't care. I don't care. I don't care. It is quiet.

"What are you staring at? What's got into you lately?"

I look down. I can see sandals and a dress, green and white with red blobs. It's a skin like a snake, like a cocoon. Inside it is dark.

"Nothing," I say.

Leaving

There isn't anything to say. There aren't any words in my head. I'm not glad anymore. Nothing hurts. It's like watching the dentist drill my mouth after I'm already frozen. It's the same too because a part of me is waiting for the hurt to start. I think that. I think how it is harder not to know when the pain is coming because then you're always waiting. I think about dentists and Dr. Enaharo and how Bill got bitten by a dog in his waiting room and they weren't certain if it was rabid or not so they couldn't decide whether to give him twelve injections in his stomach and he was only four. Then I realize something. If a dog wants to bite someone, it bites Bill. If there is a poisonous caterpillar, he puts his hand on it. If there is a germ that goes down your ear, it goes down his ear. I don't know what it means. The boat blows its horn.

Dave and I shake hands. It is one sharp shake. Our third fingers are curled into our palms but the secret signal feels like something I remember how to do from a long time ago. My legs are crossed over each other so my shoes look like they are on the wrong feet. I am wearing the strawberry dress. Dave is looking at her sneakers.

Jerry says, "See you later, alligator," and Bill says, "In a while, crocodile." My mother and father kiss Mr. and Mrs. Lee. Then we walk up the gangplank, which is really a huge white sheet of metal with ridges on it. We stand on the deck and the Lees stand on the ground. I can smell the tar bubbling. They are a family and we are a family. My father has his arm around my mother. I think about Red in a cage in the cargo of an airplane. They gave him an injection so he won't bark or be scared. At the other end people he doesn't know will come and put him in a kennel for quarantine. Inside the cage he has my mother's dressing gown and a pair of each of our socks so he won't feel too lonely when he wakes up.

Now I want to know. I want to ask Dave if she ever lied to me. I want to lean over the railing and shout to her. The railing presses in my belly. It is hot on my hands. It matters. It does matter. Dave. Dave. But they are standing on the ground with their hands over their heads and the boat is making a huge sucking in the water as it pulls away from the dock. I look at her until she is a pale blur on the tarmac. I ask her in my mind over and over but when I think I hear her answer yes, I know I can't tell if that's really what she's saying because it's what I want her to say.

My mother says, "God, I hope I don't get sea sick. This reminds me of when we left Hong Kong." She is leaning on the railing, looking sideways at me. My father is finding the cabin. We are outside the harbor now. "You were just a baby, not quite a year and a half. There was a typhoon. Everybody was dreadfully sick, even the crew. The waves were bigger than the boat. It was terrifying. But you just lay there in your cradle and rocked with the storm and gurgled. You didn't cry once. You weren't frightened at all."

I wonder if she is lying. I wonder that all the time now. But I can't remember. I look at her. I look at her lips and her cheeks and her eyes. Her lips are smiling. They are making words. They say, "What shall we do for the fancy dress contest?"

It is snowing in my head. It's snowing so hard that when I look behind me there aren't any footprints. The whole boat is white like an iceberg. We're going north. We're going away. I'll never see Dave again, or Christine, or Michael. I say it over, I'll never, I'll never, but I can't feel anything and it's silent inside like the snow has settled over everything. I want to shout but I can't, I can't make any sound come out of my mouth.

Ship

At dinner I start to laugh. I am eating spaghetti with the other children. The sweet red sauce makes my throat hurt. They are looking at me. I don't know their names. Their faces look like mushrooms. The laughter pushes through my belly, huge hoops of it squeeze through. It is too big for me but it doesn't stop. Bill is sitting next to me. He doesn't stop eating. Like a cat but smoother, he goes "Hmmmm, hmmm." On the other side of the room at the grownups' table, heads are turning around. I can see they are looking at me, but I am still laughing. I look at the white metal walls and the paintings of old ships in gold frames and the way the legs of the tables have feet which are bolted into the floor.

A boy with blonde hair says, "What is it? Come on, what's the joke?"

Nobody knows if I am laughing at them. The laughs are like giant soap bubbles blowing out of me, one after another, but they don't burst when they touch things. They are filling the room. The room is filling with rubbery bright balls which are pouring out of my mouth. They are jostling people's feet and ankles, they fill the space between the chairs and tables. Soon everybody will drown. The bubbles are covered in rainbows. There won't be room to breathe. Everybody will be dead. The air is still pulling at my lungs but there isn't any more sound. The children are staring at me. Their eyes are glass marbles, all different colors. I try to think of something funny. I say, "A snake came up the toilet when my mother was taking a piss."

The oldest girl screams. She is wearing a bra. The oldest boy says, "That's not funny." The other children keep looking at me. There are eight of them.

"She came jumping and hopping out of the loo with her knickers round her ankles, screaming. Right behind her came the snake. It was a cobra. It went into the stack of garden chairs. They were folded up against the wall. 'Michael kill it, Michael kill it.' She shouted that over and over and Michael came with a machete. He cut off its head. My mother stood there with her drawers down. 'Michael kill it, Michael kill it.'" The girl in the bra shudders. There are bumps on her shoulders where the straps are. "It wasn't poisonous. It belonged to an American woman. She was staying in the Ikoyi Hotel and it escaped down her toilet. She cried when she heard that it had been killed. The mascara ran down her cheeks in little black rivers from her eyes. She looked like a clown. She took the body away with her. Where the head was cut off it looked like a slice of salami."

The oldest girl clutches her stomach. The oldest boy says, "That's enough now."

"Michael always kept a sharp machete," I say. Bill is wiping up the ketchup he poured on his spaghetti. He wipes it with white bread then he squishes the bread between his fingers so the ketchup oozes out and the bread goes pink. I think maybe he is on my side.

The oldest boy says, "You're weird." His voice cracks and slips sideways into a squeak. He looks around at the other children and they nod.

I pick up my fork and start to eat the spaghetti very slowly. When I am finished I take a drink of water. A white man in uniform takes away the plates. He has black hair on his fingers. He brings pink blancmange. The grownups are eating chocolate mousse. The blancmange shivers like a fat arm when I poke it with my spoon.

The children are playing ping-pong in the games room, except the oldest girl, who is sitting with her mother in the lounge. They are sitting with their legs crossed the exact same way. I think she has the curse already and she has to wear a bra. It makes me feel sick. Her mother is drinking a green liquor. My mother is drinking brandy. She is standing with the captain. He has gold tassels on his shoulders. He is talking and she is nodding. Sometimes she looks up at him. I wish Dave was here to spy with. I wish Dave was here. My mother is looking this way and scooping the air with her hand. She has seen me. I dodge back behind the doorframe. I look at my arm and then I flex my biceps. With my other hand I feel them swell. When I look at my arm against the white wall it looks brown and tough. I will go on deck alone. It is night. The water will be dark but there will be stars and dolphins like in Dave's cartoon.

The purser is coming down the stairs. His cheeks fold up over the rims of his glasses. I get thin to slide past him. He sticks his arm out.

"Did your mother say you could go up on deck?"

I nod.

"Unaccompanied children are not allowed on deck at night."

He doesn't move. I hope the skin grows up over his eyes.

"Why don't you go and play with the other children?"

I shrug.

"Or are you a young lady already?" he says. He puts his hand between my legs and pushes it up under my dress. I pull away but he is holding my arm. "Yes," he says, "yes. I can tell." He is sweating. I try to twist my arm away. I do a karate chop with my other hand but nothing happens. "Come on now," he says, "young ladies like it. I can tell you do."

His lips are big and wet. I bend my head down and bite his wrist. He loosens his grip. I run down the corridor and down the stairs to where the lounge is but all the corridors look the same, they are all metal and white, but then I see my mother and father, they are walking down the corridor.

"Oh there you are," says my mother. "I wondered where you disappeared to."

"What was all that about at dinner?" says my father.

"Nothing, I was just laughing."

"Well, I think it's rotten that they won't let you sit at our table," says my mother. "Is the food awful?"

I nod. We go in and get Bill from the games room. He is sitting in the corner looking at the monopoly set. When he stands up I see two ping-pong balls like eggs where he was sitting.

"There they are," says the oldest boy. His hair is sweated onto his forehead from bossing everybody about.

"What a handsome boy," says my mother.

I grin at Bill. His eyes are almost closed. He looks like he is walking in his sleep. We walk together and my mother and father walk behind us. My mother's heels make the corridor echo. We don't know anybody on this boat and nobody knows us. We are a family. We go down stairs. The walls of the corridor get narrower. The laughter is starting in my belly. I run ahead of us. I am watching us walk toward me. We are a family.

Cycle IV

****

Harvest of Ghosts

1965–1968

Beach

On the beach she lies with her mouth open. Her lips are wet, as if she has been licking them in her sleep. Bill and Dad are far down the beach. I can see the kite, a red diamond in the blue sky with a yellow tail. I know the string I can't see leads down into their hands. I can't see them either. My father ran down the beach on his long hairy legs, the kite stumbling behind him till it swung up into the air, and Bill ran too. I can hear the waves, I can hear her snoring, the breath catching in her throat. The hairs on her lip are pale yellow. One arm is behind her head, the skin in her armpit pale and naked like chicken skin. Her eyes are very still under the eyelids. She smells sour and heavy, like milk that's gone off. She doesn't know I'm here. Her breasts point in two different directions. They lean away from each other. Her legs are covered in short sharp hairs like little spines. Her belly shivers when she breathes. More hairs climb out of her bikini bottoms. I'm going to hit her. I see my fist above her, ready, my fist going down into her belly, sliding in and in, up to my elbow. I have to pull it out but I can't. She is sticking to my skin. She'll swallow my hand if I hit her. There's a piece of chicken in between her teeth. After meals she takes a piece of cotton, wraps it around two fingers, pulls it tight. She saws in between each tooth. I feel sick. She's a whale, her belly's the mouth. All the food in the ocean goes into her mouth. She puts her mouth over the whole ocean and sucks and there isn't anything left in the sea, the water is thin and empty. "You're disgusting," I say to her belly, "you're dirty. I hate you." Her eyes flicker. They open.

"Hello darling." She reaches for the tube of Ambre Soleil.

I screw the cap back on the tube. My hands are greasy. I wipe them on my thighs. Sand sticks to my hands, my thighs. I can't get it off. In the sky the kite is turning and turning.

"Thank you, darling." Her voice is muffled. She's lying on her belly now. The sand is white under her head. Her hair is black and the sand is white. It is like a cloud, thick, moving, the sand, like steam. I can't stop looking. Something's happening to the sand. I have to see. I see the dark between the grains, thousands and thousands of dark pores in the sand. It's breathing, swelling and sinking, the whole beach a skin, hot and salty, the waves breathing harder. Dada dada. Come home. Dada come home. Dada. Mummy in bed warm mummy salt smell mashed potatoes belly big and warm mummy playing castles. Mummy pushing up and down, hairy scratch on my tummy. Let me go, Mummy, Mummy. She is crying funny. Fists on her belly, fists. Mummy let me go go down drown breathe her skin Mummy in. She cries out. She lies still. She lies dead. Mummy. Mummy.

I am running down the beach. The kite is laughing at me, high in the sky turning figures of eight. My feet sink in the sand. It burns. Burning. Dirty. Dirty. I run until my feet touch the wet sand. I run. Each time my foot touches the sand, it pushes me forward and up into the air. My feet are running, I am standing still.

The wind is in my hair, the roar is in my ears. I run until my stomach hurts then I dig a hole in the ground and I lie in it. I pile the sand back over me. My toes stick up. When I wriggle them the sand crumbles. I want the sand to look smooth, as if nobody is there but it doesn't. I run again in the opposite direction. I feel something sharp in the sand. I look behind me. There's blood in the sand. I run looking back, there's more blood, there's blood everywhere I run. It's my blood. Everyone can see where I've been, like a map of an expedition, a line of stitches in the sand, they lead right up to the umbrella.

My mother is sitting up. She is wearing her bikini top. Dad and Bill are there. I stand on the edge of her towel.

"Where were you?"

"I went for a walk."

"What's that on my towel?"

I want to hear her say, "Blood." It's my blood.

"What?"

"That."

"Oh." I look down. The blood on the edge of her towel is a dark flag. "I must have cut myself."

Harbor

The motor turns and dies, turns and dies. He pulls the cord until it catches. He stands up, smiling. The harbor is blazing behind him. He's cut out of the red sea like a huge dark statue. We're sitting in the boat at his feet, looking up at him. He doesn't have a face. Father, I think. He's my father, making the word like a hand reach up to his head, touch the skin there, warm and real, the dark coming in around us and the drumming now the Harmattan's come. Out in the deep harbor the liners move like giant jeweled women. We have to stick to the shore, the thick rotten smell, the shacks without sewers, children with their belly buttons sticking out standing at the water's edge. It's too dark to see them but their eyes follow us, my father standing at the wheel, steering. In the settlements they dance, they cut off chickens' heads with silver machetes, the chickens run around, headless and bleeding, children chasing after, the chickens leaving a map of their blood in the ground, the broad, brown, cracked feet smudging it, dancing through, singing like a growling from the ocean, clapping like the ground's heart beating in the dark where we can't see. The chug of the engine cuts a line through that sound that goes on and on like breathing. My father is steering us home.

Pole

The cold, the dark, the cold, the dark. What comes next? Start again. Captain Scott. No. *Due south of Tierra del Fuego lies the South Pole. Tierra del Fuego means Land of Fire in Spanish. The South Pole is cold and dark. Not all the time. In June and July it is dark. In December you go blind from the sun. Ice cracks under your feet. On the South Pole winter is in July and December is summer. South of the equator everything is back to front.*

Husky dogs have no smell. They lack the glands other dogs have. So they can live in igloos with the Eskimos without smelling. Captain Scott took huskies to the South Pole. They all died.

Christine comes in with a basket of T-shirts and socks. She opens the drawers and begins to sort out Bill's from mine. Under the armpits of her dress there are dark circles. I put down my pen. I turn around in the chair so my legs are on either side of the back, and rest my chin on it.

"Christine," I drawl, "whaddya think about five men who died looking for the South Pole? They wanted to eat each other because they got lost and anyway all there was was ice and their toes fell off, it was so cold."

"What?" she says. She keeps on picking out T-shirts, pinching their shoulders between her big fingers, then letting them drop so they come out in perfect squares. I can't figure out how she's doing it.

"Captain Scott and his team. They wanted to be the first men to go to the South Pole."

"What they going to do when they get there?"

"Stick a flag in it I guess. They have to find it with a compass anyway. Maybe the stars. I mean it isn't anything."

She shakes her head. She looks like she might laugh but she doesn't. I want her to. Suddenly I don't know if she knows where the South Pole is. "It's all ice," I say, "down there past Tierra del Fuego."

She looks hard at me. "You think I don't know where the South Pole is?"

"No. I was just thinking aloud. When you were at school did you have to do projects?"

She stops folding. She is holding my red and blue and white T-shirt in front of her. It looks very small against her dress. She takes a deep breath and stands up straighter.

I wandered lonely as a cloud
That floats on high o'er vales and hills,
When all at once I saw a crowd,
A host, of golden daffodils;
Beside the lake, beneath the trees,
Fluttering and dancing in the breeze.

Continuous as the stars that shine
And twinkle on the Milky Way,

They stretch'd in never-ending line
Along the margin of a bay:
Ten thousand saw I at a glance,
Tossing their heads in sprightly dance.

The waves beside them danced, but they
Out-did the sparkling waves in glee:
A poet could not but be gay,
In such a jocund company:
I gazed—and gazed—but little thought
What wealth the show to me had brought:

For oft, when on my couch I lie
In vacant or in pensive mood,
They flash upon that inward eye
Which is the bliss of solitude;
And then my heart with pleasure fills,
And dances with the daffodils.

"'Daffodils,' by William Wordsworth." She pauses then she waves the T-shirt in front of her like a matador's cloak. She grins. I think she's going to wave it over her head like a flag. The Union Jack. I know she already figured that out. She stops and then she says very slowly: "A daffodil is a yellow flower, twelve to eighteen inches high, which blooms in spring."

"You remember that whole poem and you never even saw a daffodil?"

"Every morning for a whole dry season," she says, "we stood up and recited it. Miss Hargraves was the teacher in the CMS. She said, 'Children, poetry is most important.'" Christine's lips are twisting. Miss Hargraves has a Scottish accent. "'A beautiful poem like "The Daffodils" may flash upon the inward eye, bringing solace and joy in time of trouble.'" Christine puts her finger to her lips and then she looks from side to side. "'Children,'" she says, pauses again, "'who can tell me, what is the inward eye?'" She glares at me. I sit up straight.

"I don't know Miss Hargraves."

"Well, hazard a guess." Her voice sounds like a snake.

"It can't be either of the real eyes so it must be another eye." I scratch my head slowly and frown deeply.

"Do not scratch your filthy lice in my classroom. Stand up," she says. She is walking towards me. "How many times have I told you." She is breathing in my face. "Hygiene and personal discipline are of the greatest importance."

She waves the T-shirt in front of my nose and sticks out her chin. She begins to laugh. I watch the laugh spread across her face like wind on a lake. I laugh too until there are tears in my eyes. She is shaking her head and still laughing as she folds up the T-shirt and puts it in the drawer.

I stop laughing. "What is the inward eye?"

"The inward eye," she says, "is the eye of the imagination. For seeing things when they are not in front of you."

"Like the South Pole," I say, wiping my hand all the way across my forehead and flicking the sweat away. I am back in the bar, my six-shooter at my side.

Christine says, "Do your homework."

I pull my watch out of my vest pocket and look at it seriously. "Yup," I say, "reckon I better." I turn back to the desk and write, *The South Pole isn't any different to look at than any other place in the Antarctic but that's where Captain Scott had to plant his flag so everyone would know it belonged to England. Not to penguins.* I know I'll cross that bit out later.

Christine stands in the doorway holding the empty basket in front of her. "Schooling is very important," she says. "Myself I had to leave before I reached the sixth standard so I never got my certificate." Then she is gone. I hear her feet squeaking on the tile floor. I can see her white dress sailing down the corridor. Her arms are the masts. She steps on a white tile then a black then a white. Suddenly I can see the Pole. It's made of light. It runs through the center of the earth and the earth spins on it, blue and shining, in the middle of space.

Death

"Christine, when did the war begin?"

She is hanging clothes on the line outside the kitchen window. She hangs up my red T-shirt. Daniel is inside with his knives. He is a Hausa.

"Two weeks ago they are calling it that," she says, stooping to the basket in the grass, wringing the sheet between her hands so it coils and stiffens.

"But it was happening before?"

"Long time before."

"In the north?" I remember the pictures, the people in long lines walking south. "A year ago?" I want to know when it happened. The line is stretching longer and longer, the people like ants crawling down the country, a dark line like blood flowing down. It won't stop. Something's going to happen and everybody's waiting but then it's happened and I didn't see when. It's like the moonflower the first time I watched it. I never saw it move but it opened. I wanted to see it happen but I couldn't. I waited and waited but it happened without me seeing. Everything keeps happening and happening. "War," I say, "war." Wars are declared. In war there are two sides and a line in between them. They shoot across the line. The soldiers shoot each other and their blood goes into the ground.

The basket is empty now. Christine is going to go away. She is going to go. "Christine, tell me a story. Please?"

She looks at me, about to say something then she takes a breath. We go upstairs and we sit together on my bed.

She says, "The year my grandmother's sister was dying she told us the stories. She was the oldest woman in the village. Every night she told us a story so we would remember and we would know how to live. She told us stories of every animal and of our ancestors and of the spirits and of her own young days and each story she told she was a little thinner. We were children mostly, smaller than you. Already many in the village were going to the towns, to Enugu and Port Harcourt and even Lagos. She told us we must remember what we can and hold it in our bellies. She told us when we are old, in the year of our dying, we will tell the stories to our grandchildren, as many as we remember, and even if they are pieces, the stories, when we tell them we will hear what she is hearing now, which is a story all the stories are a part of, and although we cannot remember everything and the stories are lost and broken, we will hear it too like a song in the morning from far away, and the day we die we will go to that place where the singing is, where she is going now."

Christine is silent. I wait. She is looking in the inside place. After a long time she moves. I don't want her to go.

"Why do people die?"

"Why?" She looks at me. "You think if you understand everything it will make it better?"

I keep looking at her. I want to remember her face exactly.

“Well,” she says, “this is one story my grandmother’s sister did tell me, which is of the origin of death. Now you see when God created the world He left the creatures to choose if there should be death or not. There were two groups then, the humans and the animals. God asked the two groups to decide among themselves whether death should be in existence. All the living creatures gathered in one place and the majority of them decided there should be no death. A few others, led by the crocodile, maintained that there should be death, but since they were the minority group they kept quiet.

“Now the dog was sent to inform God that there should be no death. On the way he saw some bones and he stopped to eat them. Now the bones were so sweet he forgot his mission to God. The crocodile saw him eating and immediately he sent the frog to tell God that there should be death. This the frog did.

“Now when the dog finished with the bones he remembered what he was supposed to be doing and he ran as fast as he could to God with his message but God told him he was too late and that He had already created death.

“That is how death came about.”

I look at Christine. She looks back.

“But where did the bones come from?”

She doesn’t say anything, just looks.

“I don’t understand.”

“A lot of things nobody understands,” she says.

She gets up and goes downstairs. I hold the picture of her face in front of me, her wide cheeks with the diagonal lines, and the exact flare of her nostrils. I look at her lips, plump and purplish like an eggplant, and her ears, large and plain, like a leaf or a stone. Her grandmother was Akueke who never told. Her eyes are brown and orange and gold. Her eyes see everything and she laughs and is sad and gets angry, her face like water with the wind on it, and sometimes her face is still like a pool by a cliff and she travels to her secret place and her eyes are dark then too, watching what she watches in silence. I think I will remember everything exactly and one day I'll put it all together and it will fit like a jigsaw. There won't be any piece missing.

Malaria

The fever is gone. My bones are thin. Where is Christine? There are footsteps in the hall. Christine. Christine. She is holding me in her arms, my cheek against her warm breast, soft, pressed up against my cheek, warm in my belly. She is holding me. I close my eyes, red like a plum and warm, redder and redder, the smell of her, her white dress pepper smell, red pepper, the smell of her armpits. I want to burrow into her, her hands big and hot on my back, her big arms are wrapped around me. Christine. I'm tired. I can't move. I'm too tired.

The handle on the door turns. It wags down like a duck diving, the metal squeaks. The door is pushed open, wider and wider, swinging across the floor, it hits the stop, thump against the rubber. My mother walks in, she steps into the room, she steps off the black and white tile into the room and she walks to the bed. She sits on the side. I stiffen my body so I don't roll into her where the bed suddenly slants down. She is wearing a red dress. My eyes are closed. I don't want to see her eyes. She smells of iron. She has come to see me. I am sick. She puts her hand on my belly.

It is warm. It takes away the ache. It moves under the sheet, down, down there. It moves up and down, down there. The ache in me is melting, is running together like mercury, a broken thermometer on a table, the drops pushed together in a bigger and bigger drop, shining silver, together. It is moving, pulling me. I look at me in the drop. I am shining. My face is screaming. It is bent. I am watching. This is weird. I am sick. My mother is sitting at my bedside. I am sick. My mother is sitting. Her lips are moving. "Dirty," she says. "Dirty girl." I watch my body. It is twitching like a fish. I am stabbing her. I hold the knife high in the air. It is silver. I can see my face in the blade. Her dress is red. The dark stain hardly shows. I am stabbing her over and over. She is touching me. All of me is running into her hand where she will hold me. I am stabbing her. Hold me. Hold me.

Man

I am grown, a tall and handsome man. Muscles stretch across the bony plate of my chest. My arms fill the sleeves of the jacket I wear. My shoulders are thick with muscle. At any step my toes can push me from the ground. In one enormous stride I might be anywhere. A leopard looks at me. His spots ripple like wind in the leaves. I look in his yellow eyes. I am not afraid. I am a man. I run the marathon. My bronzed body oiled, I run. In Sparta I am a hero. My body coils and hurls the javelin. The people cheer and then are silent as the javelin travels up, up towards the sun. A thin dark pole, it will pierce the sun. The people are afraid.

Spy

Spies learn to be invisible. They have to. It's a lonely job. Everybody wants to get a spy. So how do you become invisible? It's more than clothes and haircut and accent, though of course you must speak the people's language perfectly." I linger on "of course." My voice deepens. "It's a way of life, not just a collection of skills."

Dave smirks. I frown, pause, turn toward the window, my hands behind my back. When I turn to face her again I say, "It goes deeper than just dressing up as the kind of person nobody notices, a newspaper vendor, a traffic policeman, a servant. You must think invisible. You must wrap invisibility around you like a cloak." For a moment I think of Sherlock Holmes but he is different. "Stand on the edge of a crowded room and think invisible. When you breathe the air, think 'I am air,' when you listen to the sounds of the room, think 'I am these sounds.' Find the sounds in your body which match the sounds of the room. When a room is silent, listen to the silence in your body. You could walk through fire like that, finding the fire in your body." I pause. My voice is weary when I say, "Class dismissed. After luncheon we will discuss torture."

Dave stands up very straight. She turns sharply and walks out of the door, closing it behind her. When she comes back in she is grinning. "Torture again," she says.

"It's very important," I say.

After we've eaten we go back up to her room. I say, "It's your turn." She sits me on the chair and ties my hands behind my back. She ties my feet, one to either side of the chair. The knots are small and tight. She is good at them and quick. I know I can't get loose.

"Well?" she says. She is standing behind me. "What do you have to tell me today?" She hisses a little when she speaks. I hope she will do better today. I don't want to laugh. I don't say anything. Her hands grab the back of the chair. I begin to fall backwards. My body pulls forward but I can't go anywhere. She slams the chair forward, then back again, further this time. Her face is upside down.

"Well?" Upside down her eyes are smiling but then they go hard. I look into them. "Well?" Her voice is thinner. "Sooner or later," she says, "you will tell me everything. You could save yourself a lot of pain." She slams the chair forwards. "Have it your way," she says. She comes and stands in front of me. She looks at me with her head to the side. She is measuring me. Waiting is the hardest part. She knows that. "I'm going to tickle you," she says. I try not to think about where she will go first. I will myself not to laugh. She slides her hands into my armpits. I can't stop at first but then I breathe very slowly and I don't laugh so she tickles my stomach. I still don't laugh. Then her hands are everywhere, they are crawling all over me, one hand is tickling inside my thigh, she knows that is the worst place. It doesn't tickle, I say over and over in my head, it doesn't tickle. "Ready to tell?" she says. I don't say anything. I'm not laughing. All I can feel is her fingers prodding me.

"Well," she says, "this is a pleasant challenge for my skills." She sounds like me. She goes in the closet, then she is standing behind me. She puts something around my eyes. It is her bandanna. She ties it tight. I feel a rush of wind in my face. She is testing. If I flinched I could still see. The door opens and closes. I don't know if she is still here. I make my mind go around the room very slowly to feel if she is anywhere. She isn't. I am waiting. I count my heart beating. Every time I get to a hundred I uncurl one of my fingers. The door opens. It doesn't close again. I see her mother standing in the doorway. "Dave?" I say. I can't help it.

"Hah," she says. "Ready to talk?"

I shake my head. The door closes. Dave's feet walk around and around me. I can feel her eyes looking at me. I feel warm inside and my skin feels warm. I can't make her stop. She can look at me all over. I feel as if I am floating very slowly down like a feather. It's not my fault she's looking at me. Her eyes are all around me. I am in a bubble inside a beam of light, warm like the sun, like the eye beams that come from God in the book Granny gave me. It is like a searchlight making a white circle on the dark sky and I am inside the circle and wherever the light goes, I am.

"Smiling," she says, "smiling. We'll see about that."

It doesn't matter anymore what she does. She pulls the front of my T-shirt away from my skin and drops something down it. It is hot or cold, then it is cold and wet. It slides down my belly and gets stuck where my T-shirt is tucked into my shorts. It is an ice cube melting. She puts some more down my back. My skin feels brown and warm. The cold is a long way away. "Nothing," she says. Her voice sounds doubtful. "I'm going to have to beat you then, aren't I?"

I shrug my shoulders. When she doesn't move I shrug them again. She puts something cold against the inside of my leg. It is her knife.

"Do what you will," I say, "I'll never tell."

I feel a pull on the rope at my feet and then it goes loose, the same thing happens at my hands. "Stand up," she says. I don't move. She slaps my thigh. "Stand up." I stand up. She takes my shoulder and moves me a few steps then she pushes me down and down so I am lying over the chair, the wooden edge pushed into my belly. My eyes go red. I feel all my blood sliding towards my head. Something hisses in the air. "Well?" she says. "Well?"

"Nothing," I say. "You'll get nothing out of me." I know she is afraid. The belt hits my ass hard. It stings. My body jerks. She hits again and again. I fall into the gaps in between, waiting for it to hit again. When it hits it hurts but it isn't like stubbing my toe. It is a different kind of hurt, after the sting it feels good. I feel the edge of the chair on my belly. I'm not scared anymore. I'm floating again. I'm not scared waiting, it's just a feeling. I am floating and it's like swimming very slowly in warm water. I'm waiting. Time stretches out wider and wider. How long have I been waiting?

"Get up," she says. "Take off the blindfold."

I don't want to. I don't want to see her face. She pulls it off my head. "Ow." It hurts where my hair got tied into the knot.

"Class is over," she says. "Dismissed."

"I have to pee," I say and I go to the bathroom. Everything looks as if it is wrapped in light. I stand on the toilet and look at my ass in the mirror. There are red lines from the belt. It doesn't make sense. I know it is wrong. I wonder if this is what Jerry feels when Mr. Lee beats him. He doesn't yell either. But it's different; he doesn't make it happen.

The chair is back at the desk and the belt and the rope have gone. "I put the rope in your bag," she says. I nod. It is clothesline my mother gave me to practice tying knots for Brownies. I look at Dave but she isn't looking at me.

Doll

In the middle of the night the lights are on. Bill is pretending to sleep. I know when he is pretending because his face gets smooth and quiet. When he is really asleep he has two wrinkles between his eyebrows like he is thinking hard. He woke up screaming. My mother came in. She bent over him. She said he could come and sleep in her bed. He shook his head. Now he is pretending to sleep. She is outside on the landing. My father is at the war. I am keeping watch.

I watch Bill. His face is soft like the bones haven't decided what to be. He's little I think and the blood beats harder in my chest, like a red fist thumping. I hear her hand on the door handle. Everything gathers inside me in a ball in my belly burning no, no, no. Then I am quiet, all of me pointing in one direction like a snake hunting a lizard; my eyes are dark. If I look at her she'll be stunned, she won't be able to move. I see her then like a photograph, she's standing against a white mantelpiece, nothing in her eyes. They are empty and black. She is thin, her skin pale. Now I can see the whole room, the red curtains, Dad and Grandpop and Ma all looking at her. Their eyes are pointing at her. She can't move. I want to tell them to stop. She's afraid. I'm standing on Grandpop's knee. It's my fault. I took off my clothes. I made her scared. My shoulders are crimson and green and purple, the colors of fish under the sea. "Look at this child. Just look at this child." The room is filling up with water. They're going away. I shouldn't have told. She can't see me anymore. I'm in the bathroom in the corner. The walls are dark green all around me. My stomach's a hole, it's eating me. The cold dark is sucking away my skin.

I drink water from the toilet. I can't cry anymore. She's never going to see me again. My skin is falling into pieces. She's walking in the kitchen. It's getting dark again. I hear her footsteps outside. She opens the bathroom door. She comes inside. She pulls up her dress and she pees. She can't see me. I crawl across the floor. The air is thick and slow. I touch her ankle, it's warm. I try to reach my fingers round it. It goes away. Then I'm in the air. She is holding me. Her belly is warm. She's got a hairbrush. She carries me to the bed and she puts me down on the bedspread. It has knots in it. I don't have any clothes on. She's holding the hairbrush. She's pushing it down there. She pushes and pushes.

I'm looking down on me. I'm little. Little girl on the white bed. There's red on the white. There's blood in between her legs. She's a doll, a dead doll, a doll on the bed, a doll with blood who keeps saying "mummy please mummy please mummy please come back mummy don't go away mummy come back mummy don't go away mummy."

She's walking away, her feet walking down the landing, down the black and white tiles, away. Mummy. I look at Bill, his face wrinkled as if he used to be bigger but now he's shrunk, pulling his skin back in around him.

"Bill," I say. He doesn't answer. I sit in the light, with the dark at the windows pushing to come in. It's the ocean, I think. This is a ship in the dark, all the portholes shining, bright as a diamond necklace like the Titanic on T.V., all the women in gowns, and outside you know the iceberg is getting closer and closer, and when they sink do the lights carry on shining on the way down? I see it sinking down through the layers of the sea, the water growing darker, the lights going out one by one. It's quiet now. I get up and turn off the overhead light.

Back in bed I watch the Titanic settle on the seabed. There are giant jellyfish lit up from the inside with filaments like light bulbs only they are emerald and purple and crimson, they float up and down in the dark over the dark body of the ship.

Oil

"Yes Matthew."

"I brought these in, Mr. Rice, to show the class. They're crystals from the oil well."

"Good. Put them on my desk so everybody can come and look. Would you like to tell us more about them?"

Matthew goes to the front. He will look the same when he is forty, like a mushroom with tiny brown freckles. He's gotten taller since third grade but he hasn't changed. It's like there's a big quiet field inside him and black and white cows are grazing there and they always have and they always will and his eyes are brown like the cows' eyes.

"They come from deep in the earth, from the heart of the planet," he says. I can feel Christopher trying to get me to look at him. If I do we will giggle and get sent out. "You drill down looking for oil with a tube like a mosquito's proboscis, you suck up segments of rock and soil at different depths to see if it's the kind where you find oil."

I think of oil spurting up the narrow tube, black and shiny and thick, bursting out of the top like a weird flower.

"Who knows how oil is made? Yes, Anna."

"It comes from forests and swamps from millions of years ago which rotted and got buried and pressurized by all the weight of the earth on top of them and the heat from the center and they turned into oil."

"Very good. Thank you."

I picture the great black pools trapped in rock deep in the earth, and the little people on the surface trying to find them, sending down needles, just missing or stopping too short, and the oil looks like a creature, a whale, who got trapped when the sea turned to rock. It happens again, the panic like a hand squeezing my stomach. I can't remember. I can't remember if I answered Mr. Rice in American or English. I only just spoke and I can't remember. I look at Matthew's face and Christopher's and Caroline's. They just look ordinary. They would have laughed if I had talked in English, like they did in the beginning. "Tomahto." "Dew yew have a butler?" But then I learned. I didn't have to think. It was easy, except sometimes when Dave came to my house. Then my mother would say, "Don't speak in that dreadful American accent," when Dave was in the bathroom, but mostly I didn't have to think about it. I don't think I did. The panic is thin and sharp, it's in my chest now. It's like everything that happens is a piece of cloth which is stretched too tight and the fibers are beginning to give, it's getting holes in it, more and more, and I can't stop it. I watch the holes quietly forming. It's not like they're being ripped but like the material isn't strong enough, it's just giving up. I don't know where this picture comes from either except I think maybe I made a kite once with my father. I can see him frowning as he fastened the cotton around the frame, I can see the way his lips fade into the rest of his skin and they look young and he is reading the instructions. We put water on the cotton so it is wet so it will shrink tight on the frame, but when I go back and look it has holes in it. I'm not sure if I remember this or if I am making it up.

It is my turn to look at the crystals. They are tiny perfect cubes like box kites, and they are pink and yellow and blue like rainbows. They come from deep in the earth near the dark waiting pools of oil. I never thought of rainbows underground. The colors make me smile. I think of Granny and the Isle of Man and I think maybe she had a pot with sugar in it on the table and the sugar was pink and yellow and blue and she called it rainbow sugar. I don't know. "They're neat," I say to Matthew. He is smiling. His teeth are milky white. I want to take some of the crystals but he doesn't stop looking at them. I want to carry them in my pocket.

In the corridor Matthew comes up to me. He hands me a little paper package. "Here," he says, "because they made you smile for the first time in a while."

"He's a poet and he knows it," I say to Christopher. But I say, "Thank you," to Matthew and I smile. I can feel tears in the corners of my eyes. I put the package in my pocket and I go into the bathroom. I open it, careful not to lose any. They shine there quietly, like tiny butterflies. He gave me lots of them. I pick one up and look at the light through it. It comes from deep down in the earth. I put it on my tongue. It is sweet. Tears are running down my face now. It is dissolving in my mouth. It's sugar. He lied. He lies too. I want to run laughing. I'll never tell anyone.

Under

The war is happening all day long all the time. My finger moves in the warm sand, around and around, the grains parting, spreading out behind my finger like the wake from a boat. All day long it is happening. I can't see it. It's a long way away but it is happening. Christine knows. She knows it all the time. The killing ghost is living in the place she used to go when she went away in her eyes. Christine didn't believe it but she went and she saw her. She touched the ghost's arm in Biafra and the ghost looked at Christine but she didn't kill her. She didn't kill me either. I've seen her too. She lies in the ground everywhere, waiting. If you make the wrong pattern she wakes up. I made a map with my blood in the sand so she could find me. I didn't know I was doing it. I look at the sand on the windowsill, sand from the Sahara the Harmattan brings. I've drawn the pattern again, one spiral then another going the opposite direction. My eye follows the spirals round and round, going in and out and down. My body is peeling off like layers of clothes, I am getting smaller and smaller. In the middle there is a baby with a clenched fist and in the baby's fist is a tiny piece of bone and the bone is carved like the killing ghost, square white with a hole in it. I make her open her fingers. The white and the hole get bigger. I go through. I step out of my skin like a pair of trousers. It is dark. I go looking for the place where people go when they go away. I walk in between the bodies. I am looking in their eyes for that place and the bullets are whistling and the machine guns are like drums and the screaming is singing now in that place where I am looking for Christine and my mother and my father.

From that place I can see the other world like looking through a window into a lighted room only more like lying under a glass table looking up, like lying under water, the water is smooth as glass and on top of the glass people are living, walking and talking and sitting. I think then they are like the Ibejis which are really dead but their mothers make dolls of them and feed them and dress them so the killing ghost will not come and take more people, but really everybody on top of the glass is dead anyway, is an Ibeji doll, and each doll has a twin who lives underneath with the killing ghost where I am and is alive and is singing and dancing with the music. Up above on the water I see my father and mother and Bill and me in a line, smiling, wearing bright clothes, never moving, and the sun is shining so hard on the water it's like a mirror, they can't see under.

Fancy Dress

The Yellow Rose is in the garden, laughter comes up from below. They're playing "Raindrops Keep Falling on My Head." The Yellow Rose is wearing cardboard petals which stand out from his waist like a skirt blown up in the wind, and on his head he has stamens which nod as the Bumble Bee kisses him. Her head goes backward and forward, she's sticking her tongue in and out of his mouth. He is a prince. She is my mother.

I step back off the balcony into my room. My heart is beating very slowly. I walk down the hall to my parents' bedroom, into their bathroom. I wish I didn't see. After a while I turn on the light. I look in the mirror. "I'm Jake. My name is Jake." I watch my lips make the words. "What about him? What about my father? Did he see?" My eyes are sprouting black flames. Downstairs something is happening. They are whistling and clapping and stamping their feet. I see my mother's face floating on mine, her eyes the same as mine. "My name is Jake. My name is Jake."

He is standing in the doorway. I didn't hear him. I'm not supposed to be here. He has a yellow turban and his face is colored yellow except where there are lines from his nose to his mouth and around his eyes. The lines are pinky brown where he sweated or laughed or frowned. He has a black patch for his left eye but it is pushed up onto the turban. The thin mustache sticks out in either direction like two black daggers. Around his waist he is wearing my sword and scabbard. He's a pirate on the Yellow River, which is in China. He's too tall to be a Chinese pirate. He's my father. I'm Jake. A sailor on the high seas. He's not looking at me. His eyes are coated and dull, like Red's when he gets sick. He's my father. He opens his mouth but he doesn't say anything. My belly is aching. He saw her kiss the Yellow Rose. He must have.

He says, "Your mother took off her dress at the party. She took off her dress in front of everybody." He says it over and over. His voice is flat. I want to tell him we can sail away together. I want him to stop saying it. I can see him in the mirror and his eyes are pointing at mine. I turn around. I want to find him something special he can keep. His hands are clenching and loosening, clenching and loosening each time he breathes and the air is thick with whisky, so thick it's touching me and touching him, is all between us. I'm holding my breath and my heart hurts like when I'm underwater diving for sponges, diving just to see how far down I can get, and right before I turn I grab a handful of sand and as I swim back up it leaks out between my fingers, leaving a grey-brown trail in the clear water. And now his hands are on the back of my head, pushing my face into his pirate trousers. I'm not afraid of the dark. I'm Jake. His voice is very far away. "In front of everybody," he says. He is shaking. His thing is a stick against my cheek. One hand leaves my head so suddenly I think my head flew backwards but it couldn't. He pulls it out. That's how he pees. He is holding it. He doesn't say anything but I can feel his body shaking like he's crying. He doesn't know I'm Jake. My mother knows. He doesn't know. He pushes it at my lips and I open my mouth. He puts it in my mouth. He doesn't smell like my mother. I'm afraid I'm going to throw up. He's pushing my head against his belly. The corners of my mouth hurt. I can't breathe. The thing shivers in my mouth. Something squirts out. He says, "Anna oh Anna oh Anna." I pull away hard, wriggle down and out. My cheeks are wet. I don't know if I'm crying. The words in my throat are all tangled. I'm not. I'm not Anna. I'm not but my mouth is slimy. I want to spit it out. It dribbles out of my mouth because I'm crying now, on my T-shirt, on me. Anna. I look at him, at his turban and his mustache. I don't look at the thing. He's rubbing his eyes with his fists. I say, "I want to go to sleep," but he keeps rubbing his eyes. He can't see me. I didn't see. I didn't see.

I say it over and over in my head so nothing can get in. I don't take off my T-shirt. It is stuck to me like skin. If I peel it off like a burn I will bleed. In bed I am in a diving bell, steel plates bolted together with little portholes for eyes, I am going down, down, watching the fish float up and the black water. The first fish with lamps on their heads, their faces wide and flat, swim by. An octopus tentacle curls across one porthole and then another until all I can see is its belly pulsing against the glass with my flashlight and then I am in the dark waiting for the oxygen to get cut off. I am calm. The bell is full of canaries and when there's no more air they'll all fall down, their yellow bodies like petals around me.

I wish I could remember my name. I don't open my eyes.

"Come on Anna, time for school," Christine says.

I want to cry. I don't cry. My name is Jake. Big fat smelly woman. I glare at her from under the sheet.

"What's got into you this morning?" she says.

I close my eyes again. She can't see I'm at the bottom of the ocean. My mouth is open and a yellow fish swims out and then another and another.

Christine draws the curtains. "It's time for breakfast," she says.

I get out of bed and go to the bathroom and vomit but there's nothing there. Christine splashes my face with water. She puts my arms over my head and takes the bottom of my T-shirt and begins to pull. I think I will be brave. She looks at the stain and wrinkles her nose into ten separate wrinkles. "What is this?" I shake my head. She takes the shirt off, pulling it over my ears and my mouth so I'm looking through it and everything is red and then it is off and she smells it and looks at me again and runs a bath. "A man come up here last night?" I rub my eyes with my fists and yawn. She puts me in the tub and scrubs me with the loofah but it's not hard enough. I think, if I could grow another skin, what color would it be? She washes me down there. She is looking to see if I have one too but it's inside. It's a secret. I begin to cry. The water runs down my cheeks but I don't make any noise. She puts her arm around my shoulders and she squats down so she's looking in my eyes. "What happened to you?"

"They're dead."

"Who's dead?"

I pull away from her. I slide down in the tub. "My mother and father. They are lying like this." I lie very straight with my hands by my sides and I look straight ahead until the tiles begin to swim.

"Don't you lie to me girl. What's got into you this morning?"

I want to explain to her that I stopped them, how everything went too fast and up and down and I had to stop them, and how I'm floating over them and looking down and maybe I'm dead too, I don't know.

She says, "Your father is downstairs eating breakfast. Your mother is in the garden. They're not dead. You trouble death, he trouble you." She stops and looks at me again. Her eyes are orange and brown, they're sad and angry. Her voice is warm like a patch of sunlight on my face. "Tell me what happened."

"Nothing."

Eye

Fuck them. I am curled around the eye, the red eye. Fuck them. Fuck them. My blood is beating out the words. My blood is crimson, it branches through my body like the bones in a bat's wing. It is beautiful. It is the color of pansies. Fuck. Them. Fuck. Them. I am inside. Inside the eye which is blood shot bang bang bang bang bang bang bang Aaah. Their hands are in the air, their eyes are closed, blood is spurting from their bellies. They look like they're dreaming, falling backwards, the blood pouring out between their legs. They're dead, they're dead, they're dead.

They are hanging upside down on a tree in Ile-Ibenu. They are hanging in the sun without water. The air stinks of them in Ile-Ibenu, the Country of Hatred, where I am the king. I wear a necklace of teeth, my throne is made of skulls polished smooth as ivory, they glow white in the gloom inside the palace. The pits are full of blood. A little boy comes running to my throne. He is looking for his parents. "Don't cry," I say, "I kill those who shed tears in my palace. Do not cry. They are outside. They are waiting for you." He turns and runs outside. The trees take him in their arms, the bloodstained trees. Do not cry. Do not cry.

Green

It was great fun. We were terribly poor, you know. Anna ate spinach for a year. It was all we could grow but I painted the flat wonderful, zany colors. I painted the bathroom dark green from floor to ceiling. It was like being in the jungle. Little did we know! Jack had left the Foreign Office and was working at some frightful job in Birmingham."

She never said that before. The walls were green. I remembered that. Richard is nodding. I didn't make it up. I look down at the newspaper again. The flies are covering the wounds. The children are lying dead in the pile. A girl lies broken there like a doll. She bleeds on the pile of death and people are dancing all around it. They drink cocktails and they laugh, they look in each other's eyes and they dance, they dance in the blood. A woman with no eyes takes off her clothes. She shakes her breasts. Her nipples are brown. They are like tiny fists. She sits down on the floor in the blood. A prince comes to kiss her. The bodies get more. Now the country's in half. The girl's torn apart. The soldiers are thin, their uniforms gone. They march in and in. The dolls are watching it all. Nothing hurts where they are. The dark dolls, the twins, they are watching. They are trying to watch it happen, the blood flower opening, the night thick with the stench, in the country of hatred they are trying to see when it happens.

Free

"Anna love, Mum isn't feeling well today. Wear your nice dress. Please."

"I don't want to."

"Please."

"I don't want to." There is singing inside. It is high in the mountains and early in the morning because the valleys are in shadow. Voices are singing from ridge to ridge.

I don't care. I don't care what happens. My mother is crying.

"Look, can't you see Mum isn't feeling well. Do it for me. Please."

I look at him. My head is full of singing. He is crouched down. I have never looked in his eyes before. They are grey with dark rims and pale blue rays. The voices stop. In the silence after the echoes have died away, a voice says, "He is afraid of you." I keep on looking at him. He is afraid. He is afraid of me. I smell his breath on my face. He smells sour. He is afraid. Inside there are the mountains and the singing and the shadows. I am standing on the cliff with my arms spread wide. Behind me there is steam billowing. It burns my back. I am ready to dive into the shadows like a dark lake.

"Look at Mum. For goodness' sake, Anna, please. Do what you're told."

I am laughing. I'll be alone. It doesn't matter anymore. I am thirsty for the dark. I look down. A figure with its arms spread wide and its head thrown back is floating up out of the lake. Its face is my brother's face. There are blue rings under his eyes. His eyes are closed and his face is very still, like when he's pretending to sleep, with his brown hair on the pillow and the bedside light on. I want to stroke his hair, to tell him it's O.K. I can't leave him here alone. I can't leave him with them. My heart is hot and twisting. Go away. I look at him. Go away. I pick up a stone to throw down at him but I'm crying. I can't. Go away. I'm crying now.

"Oh for God's sake," says my father, "what's the matter with you? It's only a bloody dress." His voice is relieved.

Nothing

Christine is sitting in the green armchair, waiting. The skirt around the bottom of the chair still has stains from when I flooded the house. Christine's arms lie flat along the arms of the chair, her hands hang off the ends. I never saw her sit in an armchair. Her hands just hang there. She isn't asleep. She is looking straight ahead. They hang there like the hands of the doll I broke. Her hands are bigger than both of mine. I measured once. I put my fingers up against hers. Mine were browny orange, hers were pinkish brown. The lines on her palm were dark brown. She curled her fingers down in between mine and held my hand. She lifted it up in the air. We stood there like soccer champions. There was water on the bathroom floor. Sun came in behind her and made a shadow. My shadow fit inside hers. All the time she held my hand I was growing taller. That's how it felt. I didn't make that up. "Get dressed," she said. I think it was the day after the yellow party. I don't know why we did that. Suddenly I don't know if it really happened. My mouth is slimy. It's like somebody just turned off the T.V., the picture died in my head, her and me with our hands held up. I can't see her any more. Under my feet the ship's engine throbs like a giant heart. I make the picture of her come back. She is sitting in the armchair. I walk through the veranda doors and put my hand against hers. I lift it up. It is heavy. Her eyes aren't anywhere. It's too heavy to hold. In two weeks, no ten days, the Andrews are coming to live in our house. They have three children, Sandra, Gregory and somebody else. She is waiting for them to come. I think they have freckles and red hair. They'll never be able to go outside. They'll get burnt and die. They won't. Christine will work for them for three years, just like she did for us. She'll give them baths and pick up their clothes. I want to cry. Christine is in the armchair. She is sitting looking nowhere. She went to find it in the war, the secret place. It was her home. I never asked her children's names. She couldn't find them when she went to look. She thought they were there but they were gone.

I want to tell her a story to keep inside where she can visit it, a story about butterflies, how they fly across the Atlantic Ocean every year and they know where to go even though there is nothing to show them the way, only miles and miles of water, and how in the chrysalis the caterpillar turns into liquid. Before it can be a butterfly it stops being a caterpillar. It waits in the dark without any shape. It doesn't know what will happen, how the chrysalis will tear open and it will step out and dry its wings and fly across the ocean. I want to tell Christine. I want to smell her pepper smell. The ship goes and goes. It won't stop. It's like breathing. I think of the wake of the ship, how it reaches all the way to Africa, through the harbor and the lagoon to our house where Christine is sitting and waiting, her hands dangling off the arms of the chair. The dark sea tears at the thin white line which leads from me to her. Bits of it are missing already.

I'm inside a dream. It is thick and slow. I can't make anything different. I can't make anything stop happening. There's nothing

I understand. That's what Christine's hands are like too. Someone bangs on the bathroom door. I think perhaps they banged before. I flush the toilet though there isn't anything there. I wash my hands. I look at them. I don't look in the mirror. When I open the door there isn't anyone there.

In the saloon I sit in an armchair. It is green leather. I put my arms along the rests. I can hear shouting and cheering overhead. Today they're playing the greasy pole game. You try to climb to the top of a pole which is covered in grease. If you fall down you fall into the swimming pool. It's for the grownups. There's another game where two people sit on a pole which runs across the pool. They try to knock each other off with pillows. My father says he wants to play that. There's going to be a dress up contest for the children. The saloon smells of cigars and whisky and leather. It is dark and cool. I can see me sitting in the chair the way Christine is sitting in Lagos. I'm not in Nigeria anymore. I am getting further and further away.

The Sea, The Sea

The chair and the table and the bed are metal. They are bolted to the floor. On the floor are scraps of silver foil. On the table is a fan. The fan makes the floor shiver like the sea. On the bed is a coral-colored bikini top.

"Why do I have to wear that?"

"Because you're too old to stand on stage half naked."

"How come I always could in Nigeria?"

"You're growing up. Before you know it you'll be a woman."

Her lips are crinkled. She has pins in her mouth. She is fastening silver triangles on a piece of netting. She'll wrap the netting round and round my legs.

"Why can't I be the fisherman?"

"Bill can't be the mermaid."

I am under the sea, fighting a giant octopus. It is purple and bulging in the gloom. I saw off a tentacle with my knife.

"Why not?"

"Because he's a boy. Anyway I thought you'd like to be a mermaid. You swim like a fish."

Another tentacle wraps around my belly, the suckers tearing at my skin.

"He could be a merman."

"Don't be daft. Anyway it's only for one night. It's Dad's idea. I think it's brilliant."

I am paralyzed. I can't reach my knife. I can't move my legs. I can't run. The room is getting tighter and tighter. It's going to happen. I can't stop it.

"Whatever is the matter with you? It's just a contest. It's just fancy dress."

I look at the room. The edges are blurry. I name each thing: the table, the chair, the fan, the closet. In the closet there are bottles.

I think about the bottles. I read each label in my mind. I won't listen. My mother will make a curse. She'll make me be like her. I won't. I won't ever be like her. I swear this.

My mother sniffs. "Go on now. I want to finish this. Make sure Bill has his fishing rod and his blue swimming trunks."

The deck is lined with deckchairs and grownups. They smell like sardines in oil. They will watch tonight. "I hate you, I hate you, I hate you," I say, touching each chair. In the last one Bill is lying with his eyes closed and his arms by his sides. His nose is peeling. "Mum says to get your costume ready," I say. I don't stop. I go up to the front. The prow. I work my legs through the railings. They burn my skin. "The sea, the sea," I say, "where fishes fly and horses swim and mermaids—"

"I'm bored."

"You're the fisherman." I don't turn around. "It's bound to be boring."

"I want Mum to make me a tail too."

His face is crumpled. His nose looks like the inside of something, pink and raw against his brown cheeks.

"I'll tell you a story," I say, "about a ship. O.K?"

He sits down with his legs through the railings too.

"Once there was a ship which was found adrift in the ocean six hundred miles west of Portugal. There was nothing wrong with the ship that anybody could see. The cargo, a hold full of whisky, hadn't been touched. There was a meal laid out on the table, uneaten and, some people said, still warm. But the captain and the crew and the compass and the map and the ship's boat were gone."

"Is this a true story?"

"Yes. The ship's name was the Marie Celeste. She used to be called the Amazon. And the captain's name was Briggs. He and his wife Sarah and five sailors just vanished. They left the ship but nobody knew why. And still nobody knows why."

"Maybe they all got drunk and fell overboard."

"What about the boat and the compass then? Where did they go? Listen and I'll tell you what happened."

Bill is looking at me. He's waiting.

"For a month the youngest sailor watched the sea. It was his job. He watched the sea until his head was empty like a seashell and all he could hear was the waves. He watched the wake washing away the way bird tracks melt in wet sand until there's no sign they were ever there. He watched until one day he heard a tune in the waves. As soon as he tried to hear it, it disappeared, but when he sat back it came again and then he saw, not five hundred yards away, a rocky outcrop. He rubbed his eyes. It was still there. He fetched the charts and compass. The island was impossible. He called the captain and the captain came grumbling because his dinner was getting cold. Sarah came too and the rest of the crew. 'There's an island,' said the youngest sailor, 'and a song.'

"At first they couldn't hear or see anything. They said he'd sat out in the sun too long, it had fried his brains. But he told them to spread their eyes on the horizon and to listen in between the waves."

I stop. I'm staring at the waves. Bill is too. Then I point.

"'There,' cried Sarah, 'there. See her strong arms, her shining tail.'

"'Look, look,' cried the captain. 'Her long hair, her slender shoulders.'

"The mermaid curled her tail and shook out her hair. She opened her mouth and she sang.

"'I'm going to the mermaid,' said Sarah, 'to swim with her under the sea.'

"'I'm going to the mermaid. She'll sing,' said the captain, 'I'll capture her, and she'll sing for me.'

"So he and Sarah and the crew climbed in the boat and they set out for the island where the mermaid sat, and as they rowed they sang and their voices mixed with the wind and the slap of the waves and the cries of the gulls until they could be heard no more. And that's how the Marie Celeste, once called the Amazon, came to be drifting, with no captain or crew, six hundred miles to the west of Portugal."

After a long time Bill says, "You made that up."

"So? I bet you can't think of a better explanation."

"Mermaids don't exist."

"They're famous for luring sailors to their death."

Bill gets up and walks back to his deckchair. I can't move. My eyes are watching the water. I can hear the mermaids singing. I can go there. I can live under the water. I can watch what happens on top like watching T.V. with the sound turned down. I can lie there on the bottom. The fish, yellow and orange and turquoise, will brush against my skin and nothing will hurt. If I can not care I can get there.

I am watching me watch. It's like seeing double. I watch. I watch everything. I watch me take the bottle from the closet. I gulp. It burns. I am in the metal room. I am wearing a fish's tail. I choke and drink again. I drink and drink.

There is a long passageway, a hook in my hair. It hurts. I try to punch Bill but I can't really move. "Ow," I say, "don't. Mum, he's pulling."

"Stop it Bill. Anna, be careful how you walk. I spent hours on your tail."

"Oh, the mermaid and the fisherman. How clever."

There are two Robin Hoods, a Florence Nightingale, a Roman Emperor. They rush up and down, laughing. I despise them. I feel funny behind my eyes.

I am standing on the highest block with Bill. We have been awarded first prize. The blocks are the kind used for swimming champions or bathing beauty queens.

I can't move. I can't move my legs or my arms. The clapping is a wave, it is breaking around me. It is sucking at my skin. My skin is stiff. Inside my skin is a tunnel. In the tunnel my bones are dissolving. My muscles are liquid. I am only my eyes. I turn my eyes to the faces. The faces are silver, they are shimmering. They are a silver sea. The waves are slower. I see my mother's face, her dark hair, the red lips with the extra lipstick caught in the corners of her mouth. I see my father, the mole above his lip with the hair growing out, the way his lips have no edges. I look at them where they are sitting and I think, if you weren't my parents I wouldn't like you.

Everything goes still inside. The sea is moving but inside I am a bowl of liquid which is flat and smooth. I can't breathe but I don't need to breathe because I am liquid.

> If you weren't my parents I wouldn't like you.
> The thought turns into two thoughts.
> You are strangers. I don't like you.
> The two thoughts are wings which open and close.
> You are strangers. I don't like you.

It is simple. It is so simple. I am opening and closing my wings. Below me the sea is moving, it is shining and moving. My father's face is looking up at me. His lips are moving.

"Anna," he says, "get down. Can't you see the others have left the stage already?"

"Good God," says my mother, "you stink of gin."

I am looking down at us, the four of us like a picture, the tall father, the mother with a hand on his arm, the boy with the fishing rod, the girl standing there on the block in her fish's tail.

The End